Racy pushed away from the desk and took a wide circle around him.

Not wide enough. Her bare arm bushed against his jacket as she headed for the door. The movement caused goose bumps to skate down to her fingers.

One booted foot hesitated across the threshold. A rocking country song that warned of T-R-O-U-B-L-E rang in the rafters.

Gage's arm shot out.

His palm landed against the door jamb, blocking her exit. "If you keep walking, I'm going to follow." He leaned in, his mouth at her ear in order to be heard over the loud music. "Do you want everyone to find out we're still married?"

Dear Reader,

Have you ever met someone who was your total opposite, but deep inside you shared kindred souls? Someone that conventionality and common sense said was all wrong for you, and as much as you try, you still found yourselves the definition of "opposites attract"?

Well, Racy Dillon and Gage Steele didn't just attract, they created a magnetic force that has continued to pull them to each other ever since they were teenagers. Now adults, both think they have found their place in the world, until one wild night in Vegas changes everything. And the harder they try to fix things, the messier it gets! Throw in meddling family members and a golden retriever that can't seem to remember which house is his, and you have a wacky and wonderful love story—my favorite kind!

Enjoy!

Christyne

THE SHERIFF'S SECRET WIFE

BY
CHRISTYNE BUTLER

All the characters in this book have no existence outside the imagination of
the author, and have no relation whatsoever to anyone bearing the same name
or names. They are not even distantly inspired by any individual known or
unknown to the author, and all the incidents are pure invention.

First published in Great Britain 2011
Harlequin Mills & Boon Limited,
Eton House, 18-24 Paradise Road, Richmond, Surrey TW9 1SR

© Christyne Butilier 2010

ISBN: 978 0 263 88858 4

23-0111

Harlequin Mills & Boon policy is to use papers that are natural, renewable
and recyclable products and made from wood grown in sustainable forests.
The logging and manufacturing processes conform to the legal environmental
regulations of the country of origin.

Printed and bound in Spain
by Litografia Rosés S.A., Barcelona

Christyne Butler fell in love with romance novels while serving in the United States Navy and started writing her own stories six years ago. She considers selling her book a dream come true and enjoys writing contemporary romances full of life, love, a hint of laughter and perhaps a dash of danger, too. And there has to be a happily-ever-after or she's just not satisfied.

She lives with her family in central Massachusetts and loves to hear from her readers at chris@christynebutler.com or by visiting her website at www.christynebutler.com

For my daughter, Cagney,
whose passionate and independent spirit
continues to inspire me…you are my greatest joy

and my husband, Len, who is always there to
fix things for me

Chapter One

Last week of August…

Racy Dillon swore on her daddy's grave the four-foot-tall trophy, its imitation walnut base and three tiers separated by shiny purple-and-gold columns, was the ugliest thing she'd ever seen. Thanks to her still-fuzzy brain it took a few blinks and squints before the award came fully into focus.

Yep, still ugly.

Even the winged female figure atop the highest tier looked tacky, especially with Racy's pink lace panties hanging from the five-pointed star the figure held aloft over her head.

The black brass plate read *First Place, Midwest Regionals, U.S. Bartenders Challenge, Las Vegas, Nevada,* thank you very much. She'd come here all the way from Destiny, Wyoming, to kick butt and take names.

Mission accomplished. Hangover accomplished, too.

It felt like a chorus line of jackhammers doing high kicks inside her skull. Even so, they couldn't erase last night's memory of hearing her name called out with a near perfect score. She'd made a show of tucking the prize money into the cleavage of her push-up corset and then the celebrating had started. Hey, if anyone knew how to party it was bartenders. It had begun with a round of tequila shooters and had just got better. Of course, the memories grew fainter from that point, too. It'd been years since she'd tied one on like she'd done last night.

Racy closed her eyes. Not only to erase the slight tilt of the room, but to block the sunlight sneaking past the floor-to-ceiling curtains that barred the best view of the Vegas Strip. Another perk of winning. An upgrade from a standard room to this luxurious suite for the rest of the weekend.

She stretched beneath the sheets, enjoying the coolness of the five-hundred-count cotton material on her naked skin. Grateful for the plush pillows that cradled her throbbing head, she rolled to the edge of the bed.

Damn, she needed a tall glass of ice-cold apple juice. She didn't know why, but it always cleared her brain after a night of wild—

A deep groan and movement from behind her caused Racy to freeze. Before she could move, a wall of heat and muscles spooned up against her. A jawline, complete with bristly stubble, rested against her shoulder as a heavy arm draped over her hip.

Another groan—no, it was more like a moan, then a nuzzle at her hair and the press of a mouth to her skin—before he stilled. Deep breathing relayed his trip back to a peaceful slumber. Not entirely peaceful, if the hardness pressing against her backside, and the sheets caught between their bodies, meant anything.

Oh, no. She didn't. She didn't do stuff like this anymore. In her reckless past, sure, but not now.

Racy pressed her fingers to her pounding forehead. *Think, girlfriend. What the hell happened last night?*

She remembered celebrating in one of the hotel bars. There was a slick guy, like someone out of *The Godfather,* who wouldn't take no for an answer. He'd pinched her ass. She'd slapped him. He'd raised his hand, but someone— tall, broad shoulders, killer smile—had stepped in and defused the situation.

Then what?

Shoot 'em?

She'd told the stranger who'd rescued her to shoot someone? Her mind whirled. The rest of the night was a blur of bright lights, loud music, the jangling of slot machines, and more alcohol. And him.

His face was blurry, but she recalled dark brown hair and strong hands. Hands that had caressed her body while they'd danced. Powerful arms that had carried her out of the fountain she'd insisted on dancing through. And a mouth that had delivered hot, wet, soul-stirring kisses. On the dance floor, up against a palm tree, in a taxi on the way to…where?

And Elvis?

No, it must be a dream. A bad dream. A nightmare.

Only it wasn't. And she'd brought her rescuer back to her room.

Memories flashed in her mind. The desperate need to undress. Hands tugging, clothes flying and with only her corset, denim miniskirt and stilettos, she'd gotten naked first. He'd lunged for her, but she'd slipped free. Then she was in a whirlpool tub big enough for six, pouring bubble bath into the rising water.

It had taken him longer…why? Cowboy boots. He couldn't get his boots off and she'd laughed. Laughed until he'd finally joined her in the hot, bubbly water and made her moan. In the tub, on the stairs that led to the king-size bed, beneath the snow-white sheets that had stood out against his tanned skin—

"No." The word came out a desperate whisper. She dropped her hand to her breasts and clutched at the sheet. "No, no, no."

She had to get out of this bed and away from—oh, God—she couldn't even remember his name. How was it she could recall the feeling of his mouth on her body, but not the man's name?

Reaching to remove the weight of his hand from her hip, her fingers brushed over something smooth and cool.

A wedding ring.

Racy's stomach turned, an even more vile taste filling her mouth. She'd never picked up a married man. In her line of work, she could spot them a mile away, ring or not. Married men gave off a scent of possession, of belonging to someone else and, despite the craziness of her life, she wouldn't—

Afraid she was going to be sick, she clamped a hand over her mouth. Something hard hit her lip. She pulled away and focused on the shiny gold band on her left hand. Jerking up on one elbow, she shoved her hair out of her eyes and there it was, in the same place she'd worn wedding rings twice before.

First when she'd been nineteen and stupid, then six years later she'd taken another chance on happily ever after. When that had ended after eighteen short months, she'd vowed never to grace the aisle again.

But this ring didn't look like those cheap things from the past. This one sparkled with a row of diamonds. It couldn't be real. She couldn't be married.

No, this had to be a joke.

Her gaze flew around the luxurious suite, finally landing

on the items littering the glass-top table near the double entrance doors. Bolting from the bed, she raced across the room. Whoa, not a good idea. Both her head and stomach took their sweet time in catching up with her.

She struggled to focus on her purse and the small bouquet of white silk flowers lying next to it. There was also a rolled paper tied with a pale blue ribbon, but her eyes caught and stared at a man's wallet, open to reveal a shiny law enforcement badge.

A cop?

Racy stilled and blinked hard.

Ohmigod, she had not married him.

Then it all came back to her.

A law enforcement conference and the bartenders challenge in the same hotel. The participants of both events running into each other in the casinos, bars and restaurants, the cops often in the crowds during the challenge's preliminary events, open to the public.

One cop in particular.

She'd noticed him two nights ago standing in the back, arms crossed over his chest as he'd watched the first round of the flaring competition. It was Racy's favorite part, where each bartender's personality and style came out while showing off their moves. Spinning, flipping, catching and balancing bottles, glasses and bar tools while making a variety of cocktails. At the end of her routine, he'd offered her a wink and smile. She'd impulsively blown him a kiss, which every man in the cheering crowd who'd stood between them thought was for him.

That was the last time she'd seen him until…

She grabbed the rolled paper and yanked off the blue ribbon. It unfurled and the words *Marriage Certificate* stood out in a large, elaborate font. Her vision blurred as she focused farther down the paper.

Bride: Racina Josephine Dillon. Groom—

"Good morning."

His deep, coarse growl caused Racy to spin around. The room kept spinning, and she grabbed hold of the table for balance. He sat at the edge of the bed, the sheet pulled across his lap, leaving his chest and legs bare. Elbows braced on his knees, he cradled his head in his hand.

Oh. Sweet. Lord.

Gage? She'd married Gage Steele?

"This can't be happening." Her words came out so soft he couldn't have heard them.

But he did. His head shot up and he winced. "As soon as I figure out what *this* is, I'll come back with—"

His eyes widened and locked onto her. The heat in his gaze torched her skin from her face to her toes. She realized she was standing there in nothing but her birthday suit.

Racy reached for the closest item of clothing. Yanking on a man's white dress shirt, she managed to get three buttons closed before a clean, outdoorsy scent filled her head. Gage's shirt. Even after a night in the city, it smelled like him. Like sparkling lake water, tall trees and the earth. The kind of earth you want to dig your fingers into and inhale.

"Not bad, but I like the other look better."

Gage's voice rolled across the room and caused her stomach to roll, as well. Only this time it brought with it a rush of heat. She concentrated on finishing the buttons, ignoring the paper clenched in her trembling fingers.

"What are we going to do about this?"

"There you go with *this* again." Gage brushed his hand over his face, then through his hair, causing the short brown locks to stick straight up. "Damn, I feel like crap. I'm getting too old for tequila and late nights."

Old? At thirty-two, Gage was in his prime, with the football player's body of his youth honed to lean, tight muscles. As the sheriff of Destiny, Wyoming, he carried the town's troubles on his wide shoulders without breaking a sweat.

And he'd been nothing but trouble for her since high school.

"*This* is the problem." Racy marched to the bed. "According to a piece of paper and the rings we're wearing, it seems we tied the knot last night."

Confusion filled his dark blue eyes. "We what?"

"Don't you remember?" *Please, let at least one of us have the memory.*

He snatched the paper from her hand, his brow drawing into a deep furrow. "Hot damn, we really did it."

Her stomach plummeted to her feet. "We did?"

"Hell, I thought you were kidding when you proposed—"

"What?" Racy's shriek caused both her and Gage to grimace.

"You disappeared into a jewelry store and walked out ten minutes later with a matching set of rings." He rubbed at his eyes, stopping to stare at the gold band on his hand. "Then you insisted on going to the marriage bureau for a license."

"I did?"

"After that we hit the casinos for a while. I figured that was the end of it." Gage dropped his hand and shrugged. "When you won big at poker—pretty impressive, by the way—I had to convince you I wasn't with you for the money."

She'd hit it big? The memory wouldn't come back. How much? Would it be enough? Could she really be this close to getting—

Wait. What did *he* do? "How did you convince me?"

"Are you kidding? You made me—" His voice caught and those blue eyes turned a stormy hue. "You don't remember?"

Racy curled her toes into the plush carpet, feeling like a kid caught with her hand in the cookie jar. "Bits and pieces."

"Like what?"

"Look, I'm not one of your suspects." She crossed her arms over her chest and tossed a long curl off her face with a flick of her head. "It's obvious both of us had a few too many drinks last night. What exactly do you remember?"

"I asked you first."

"I remember winning the challenge."

Gage's gaze shot to the trophy. Hers followed. A silent groan filled her chest as his eyes lingered on her panties still hanging there.

"What else?" he finally said, looking back at her.

She fought not to squeeze her thighs together beneath his dress shirt. "I remember celebrating, when a Mafia thug started hitting on me. I thought I could handle it, but then it got out of control and some guy stepped in—"

Gage's left eyebrow rose into a perfect arch.

"You stepped in, played the hero, and I bought you a drink as a thank-you."

"That's it?" The familiar tic along his jawline told her he wasn't happy. "That's all you remember?"

Most of last night was still coming back to her in brief flashes, but the memories she'd awoken to earlier were quickly becoming clearer and brighter.

The two of them, laughing and talking, dancing and kissing. Years of feuding and smart remarks forgotten as together they explored the city. Then later, back here in this room…the almost desperate need to be together.

She couldn't tell him.

Racy swallowed hard and forced herself to speak. "Yes, that's all."

Gage tossed the certificate to the bed and started to rise.

"What are you doing?"

He flexed tanned and toned muscles. "Trying to stand."

"But you can't! You're—aren't you naked?"

He pushed at the sheet. "What's a little nudity between husband and wife?"

Racy spun away, her ears filled with the rustle of bed-sheets and heavy footsteps as he walked to the far side of the bed. The large, gilded mirror over the table gave her a clear view of a strong back, tapered waist and a backside so perfect it had to be a sin. Unable to look away, she watched him pull on a pair of boxer briefs that hugged his muscular thighs and glutes, before a pair of blue jeans covered her view. Not that they made him any less tempting.

Knock it off! This isn't real. None of it.

She leaned over, grabbed the piece of paper that told her their farce of a marriage was very real, and saw him reach for the phone. "What are you doing?"

"Calling room service." He punched a button and waited, keeping busy with something in the top drawer of the bedside table. "Yeah, this is suite 3011. Please send up an order of three eggs, sunny-side up, a double side of toast, and coffee. A lot of coffee."

He bumped the drawer closed with his knee, then looked at her over his shoulder, again with the arched eyebrow. She shook her head. Food was the last thing she needed right now.

"Add a plain bagel, lightly toasted with butter on the side, and two large apple juices. Oh, can you throw in a bottle of aspirin? Thanks." He hung up and turned around. "What?"

"How…how did you know what I like for breakfast?"

He shrugged one wide shoulder and brushed past her. "We both stop in most mornings at Sherry's Diner. I notice these things."

"Where are you going?"

"To the bathroom. Do you mind?"

He didn't wait for her to reply, but disappeared through the double arched doors at the other end of the room. Racy eyed the rumpled sheets on the king-size bed. Flashes of wild, uninhibited lovemak—

No, she wouldn't call it that. Last night was sex. Pure and simple and lusty and wonderful.

"He can't know I remember. He can't."

She quickly made up the bed, then grabbed her panties off the trophy and shoved them, along with her scattered clothes, into the zippered compartment of her suitcase. Pulling out clean clothes, she dragged undies and leggings over her bottom half. She pulled Gage's shirt over her head, then reached for the ratty gray zippered sweatshirt.

She stilled. No, she couldn't put that on. Not with its previous owner about to walk back in. She doubted he'd remember, but she couldn't chance it. She yanked a T-shirt over her head as the bathroom door opened, no time for a bra.

Gage walked out of the bathroom, the marble floor of the suite's entry area cool against his bare feet. The memory of what he'd done to Racy last night—what she'd done to him, hell, what they'd done to each other—in the hot, foamy water of the huge tub took up every free corner of his still-foggy head.

But not so foggy that he didn't notice the bed, its sheets, pillows and fancy patterned comforter, all neatly in place.

His gaze then found Racy, dressed in some kind of stretchy black pants that defined every inch of her mile-long legs. Her mass of red curls, rumpled and sexy at the same time, hung past her shoulders. She wore a familiar T-shirt with faded lettering inviting him to *Drown Your Secrets, Sorrows or Sweethearts at The Blue Creek Saloon*.

Great advice. The logo with its catchy phrase had been Racy's idea as manager and head bartender at The Blue Creek. Most in town figured it came directly from her life experiences, Gage included.

So what did that make him? A secret or a sorrow? He sure as hell wasn't her sweetheart.

"I figured you'd want this back."

Racy's voice cut through his thoughts, forcing his eyes from the worn cotton material of her shirt outlining the roundness of her breasts. She wasn't wearing a bra. He buried that fact in his mind and focused on his shirt, which she held out at arm's length.

He closed the distance between them, waiting until he stood directly in front of her to take it. He was crowding her personal space, but he didn't care. Not after last night.

He broke eye contact long enough to pull the shirt over his head, not bothering to undo the buttons. It was still warm from her body. He had to bite back the groan that filled his throat.

Spotting the certificate on top of her suitcase, he jerked his head toward it. "You know, this might not be true."

Her chocolate-brown eyes grew wide for a moment. Then she blinked and turned away, reaching for the curled paper. "What makes you say that?"

"That's not a legal document. Hell, it could've been created on any computer. The marriage license from the bureau is the only official paperwork."

Racy pushed back the mass of red waves from her face and looked around the room. "So where's the license?"

"I remember putting it in—" Gage patted his jeans pockets. "Where's my wallet?" He already knew his gun was stashed in the bedside table. He always knew where his gun was.

"On the table."

Gage turned, relief filling him as he spotted the black leather wallet and his badge. He crossed the room and grabbed it.

"Wait a minute, you don't remember last night, either?" Racy's voice caused him to pause.

No, he remembered.

He remembered the absolute joy on her face when she had taken first place. He remembered finding her in one of the hotel bars, and the way she'd latched on to his side when he'd stepped between her and that jerk hitting on her. He remembered how one drink had led to many more, then the two of them slow-dancing—and how it had felt to finally hold her in his arms again.

They never left each other's side after that.

He'd gone from bar to casino to high-end boutique with her, not wanting the night to end. Then she'd appeared with the rings, insisting she had to make an honest man of him. He'd thought she was crazy, but they were both feeling so good he'd gone along for the ride. And after she'd insisted he prove his desire to still marry her, he'd done the one thing she'd never expect.

He guessed it worked.

"Gage, answer me. Do you remember us getting married?"

He tightened his grip on the wallet, turned around and found her standing directly behind him. "The actual ceremony? No. But unlike you—" he couldn't stop from reaching out and brushing his fingers against her neck "—I can guarantee the honeymoon was fantastic."

The faint bruising on her neck faded beneath the pink blush that tinged her skin. He remembered putting the mark on her—his mark—in the wee hours of the morning. He hadn't meant to. High school was the last time he'd given a girl a hickey, but her taste, her scent and her response to what his mouth was doing proved to be *his* undoing.

And he liked it there. Obviously she hadn't seen it yet and it bothered him more than it should that in less than a week's time it'd be gone.

Racy stepped away from his touch and crossed her arms over her stomach. "I don't remember a ceremony or a honeymoon. So, could you check and see if you have the license? Maybe none of this is real, maybe it's just a big—"

"Mistake?"

"Yes, a mistake." Her chin jerked upward and her hands fisted, but she didn't look away. "A misunderstanding, a mix-up, a joke someone is playing—"

"I get it." Gage cut her off.

Her words caused a sharp pain in his chest he didn't understand. So what if he'd wanted to get his hands on Racy Dillon for the last fifteen years and when he finally had, she couldn't remember a single moment?

You remember though, don't ya, pal?

Yeah, in vivid detail. Every sight, sound and smell of their time together, both in and outside of this hotel suite, was etched in his mind.

He was so screwed.

Pushing away that thought, he opened his wallet and found the folded license he'd tucked there after leaving the bureau office, never really believing they'd use it. He shook it out, his eyes scanning the words.

"Well?"

Her one-word question held so much hope, a part of him hated to reply. His pride, however, was going to take a perverse sort of pleasure in it. "Sorry, Mrs. Steele. It seems as of two thirty-three this morning we're actually hitched."

Racy sank to the sofa, eyes wide with shock. His enjoyment of her distress drained away. He could see the idea of being married to him was turning her stomach.

She finally looked at him. "Gage, what are we going to do?"

"I can't think straight without coffee and I'm hungry as a bear. We should concentrate on eating first."

"How can you think about food at a time like this?"

Racy shot to her feet and advanced on him. "This is crazy! You don't want to be stuck with me and I sure as hell don't want to be married to you."

Okay, that was plain enough. "Racy—"

"We have to figure a way out of this. Can you imagine what the good citizens of Destiny would say if we showed up at home with matching rings?"

Yeah, it'd probably cover everything from "atta boy" to "I give it six months."

"You hate me! You've felt that way since high school."

"I don't hate you."

She snorted. "I'm not even worth that strong of an emotion, huh? Fine. Then you disapprove of me, of the way I live my life, of my family. Moonshining, drunk and disorderly, petty theft, drugs…first your father and then you took great pleasure in busting my brothers, making sure that last time they got the maximum jail sentence."

"I was doing my job."

"The night my father drove that rattrap pickup into a telephone pole, you were the first one to my place—"

"I didn't want you to hear about it from anyone else."

"No, you wanted to break me…again. You wanted to see me cry over the fact my sorry excuse of a husband and my daddy were so drunk it wasn't the crash that killed them, but the both of them walking in front of an eighteen-wheeler an hour later."

"Yeah, you were so brokenhearted you didn't shed a tear."

She paused and swallowed hard. "I don't cry for anyone. Not anymore."

Before he could respond, a discreet knock came at the door. Racy marched across the room. She flung open the door and waved the uniformed waiter and his cart inside.

"Any place you'd like this?" the young kid asked with a polite smile. "The terrace is a favorite among our guests."

Gage glanced at the glass doors at the other end of the suite. Racy and him in the open air thirty stories above the ground? Not on your life. "Ah, here is fine."

He opened his wallet, but Racy snatched the bill from the cart, scratched her name on the paper inside the leather case and handed it to the waiter. "It's my suite. I'm paying."

"Yes, ma'am." The waiter retreated to the doors. "Thank you, ma'am." He disappeared, closing the door behind him.

Gage grabbed two chairs from the nearby dining table and shoved them on either side of the cart. The aroma coming from beneath the silver domes made his mouth water. He still felt like crap, but a hearty breakfast the morning after always did wonders for him. "Come on, sit."

"Don't tell me what to do."

"Fine." Gage sat. He needed coffee. Strong, black and right now. "Stand and eat. I really don't care."

"Gage—"

"Look, we both agree we need to figure out a way to fix this—"

"And keep it a secret." Racy cut him off. "I don't want anyone to know how stupid I—how stupid we both were last night."

The coffee burned on its way down his throat, but it was no more scorching than her words. Why it bothered him, he didn't want to think about. He should've known last night hadn't changed anything. The warm and fun-loving woman he'd held in his arms was an illusion.

Reality was standing right here in front of him.

"I'll call the concierge. We can't be the first couple to have morning-after regrets." Gage set aside the domes with a loud clang and reached for a fork. "What's that saying, 'what happens in Vegas, stays in Vegas'?"

The sight of a gold-and-diamond band shoved under his

nose stopped the fork midway to his mouth. He looked up, but with her chin dropped, Racy's hair covered her face.

"What are you doing?"

"Here. Take it."

"You bought it."

"I don't care." She shook her head, dropping the ring into the water goblet next to his plate. It slowly sunk past the floating ice cubes to rest at the bottom. "I don't want it. Toss it, leave it for the maid…it doesn't matter to me."

She grabbed the apple juice from the cart, her fingers gripping the glass, but it still sloshed over the rim as she headed across the suite. Seconds later, the bathroom door slammed closed behind her.

Gage rose and started after her, stopping when he heard the sound of rushing water. The mental image of his wife in the oversize glass shower, water jets pulsating against her peaches-and-cream skin, had his lower half instantly responding.

He jammed his fingers through his hair, his gaze catching on the gold band on his left hand. Tugging off the ring, he tossed it toward the cart, watching it make a perfect arc to join Racy's in the water glass with a splash.

She wasn't his wife. In a matter of hours she wouldn't even be his ex-wife. What did one call a former spouse after an annulment?

A mistake, that's what.

Chapter Two

Last week of January…

"What in the hell are you talking about?"

"There's no need to swear. Do I have to repeat myself?"

Gage stared at his little sister. Okay, not so little, but still younger than him by a decade, sitting on the other side of the aged desk that had once belonged to their father. She'd appeared in his office early this cold Saturday morning to announce she'd gotten a job. At a bar, of all places.

And not just any bar, Racy's bar.

"Yes."

"Racy hired me last night to work at The Blue Creek."

"I was at The Blue Creek last night. I didn't see you." Gage refused to concede how just the sound of *her* name got his blood racing. Damn the woman! What had she done now?

"Well, I was there and I didn't see *you*."

"I stop in most nights to make sure everything is okay."

"Yes, I can see how the big, bad sheriff waving around his badge would keep everyone on the straight and narrow."

"I stay out of sight and I don't wave—" Gage pulled in a deep breath. He slowly released it and dropped his mail to his desk, his attention fully on his sister. "Gina, what are you doing? You've got two degrees, one of which is a master's."

"For all the good it did me in the real world."

The pain in his sister's voice was evident. When she'd arrived home from England just before Thanksgiving, he'd known something was wrong. Even Gina couldn't finish a year-long fellowship in less than three months.

"Think I'm a bit overqualified to work in a bar?"

"Yes."

"Or is it I'm not pretty enough?"

Where in the hell had that come from?

Gage studied the rigid set of his sister's shoulders. Her sheepskin-lined denim jacket had once belonged to their father. With her curly hair pulled back in its usual ponytail and her gold-framed glasses, she could pass for a high school classmate of their younger sister, Giselle.

She certainly didn't look like the waitresses who, thanks to their short skirts, tight jeans and barely-there T-shirts, served up beers and burgers at Destiny's local watering hole.

Women like Racy.

Last night she'd been dressed from head to toe in black, from the stomach-baring tank top to the jeans molding her perfect curves to the cowboy boots on her feet. The only color came from her flame-red hair and the gold jewelry she wore at her ears, neck and…belly button.

The piercing was new. It hadn't been there five months ago. He should know. The gleaming diamond stud had fueled a fantasy he'd awoken from in the early morning hours, drenched in a cold sweat. Par for the course lately.

"Thank you for rushing to my defense."

Gage blinked, his sister's dry tone drawing him out of his thoughts. "Huh? No, you're pretty, you're beautiful. It's…"

"I know. The girls who work there look…different." Gina glanced down at her clothes. "What can I say? My life has been more about books than looks, but Racy said she'd help me."

"Help you?"

"She offered to give me tips on hairstyles and clothes."

Gage tried to picture his sister dressed like the flamboyant redhead. His mind wouldn't allow the visual to come to life. He leaned forward. "Gina, those girls aren't only selling booze and food. They're selling a good time. They flirt and tease—hell, Racy's even got them line dancing on the bar."

"Racy said some of her girls work to help their families make ends meet."

"True," Gage conceded, "but other than last night when's the last time you were in The Blue Creek? In any bar?"

"What does that have to do with anything?"

"Most of Racy's girls are young, single and looking for a good time."

Gina jumped to her feet. "Hey, I, too, am young, single and looking for a good time. I've had it with genius IQs and think tanks. All those years away at school, I don't even know most of the twentysomethings in this town. I want friends my own age. I want to meet guys my own age. Did you know this past summer was the first time…"

Gina's voice trailed off. She closed her eyes for a long moment, then opened them as she straightened. "I'm doing this, whether you like it or not. I came here first because Racy thought I should tell you."

"She what?"

"Racy said I should let you know about working for her."

Yeah, he just bet she did. She'd hired Gina to spite him.

From the moment they'd walked out of the lawyer's office last August and into the Las Vegas sunshine, she had taken great pleasure in either pretending he didn't exist or antagonizing the hell out of him. At first, he'd avoided the bar, letting his deputies cover both the peaceful and the more frequent not-so-peaceful watches.

Then during the baseball play-offs a free-for-all had broken out at The Blue Creek. He'd arrived in time to get in the middle of flying fists. After getting knocked on his ass, he'd looked up to find Racy consoling Dwayne McGraw, his former high school teammate. Married with six kids, Dwayne outweighed him by a hundred pounds. He was also too drunk and pissed off about his team losing to listen to anyone telling him to calm down.

Anyone but Racy.

And that'd annoyed Gage more than it should have.

"Hello?" Gina snapped her fingers. "You still with me or have I shocked you into silence?"

"I'm here." He blinked away the memory. "Look, I can fix this."

"There's nothing to fix!"

"I can talk to the principal at the high school." He started making notes on his desk calendar. "See if they have any openings. Or I could check with the University of Wyoming—"

Gina slapped her hand on top of his, forcing the pen from his fingers. "I want to meet people my own age, not teach them. Stop trying to solve a problem that isn't there and stop telling me what to do. Geez, I'm twenty-two, not twelve."

He looked at his sister. "I'm not telling you what to do."

"You could've fooled me."

A deep sigh gutted from his chest. He couldn't help it. Whenever he looked at Gina he saw long braids and chunky braces. "Promise me you'll be careful and not do anything crazy."

"Like dancing on the bar?" The look in his sister's eyes matched one he'd seen many times before, both in the mirror and in the faces of their siblings. Determination.

"Gina—"

"I've got to go." She cut him off. "I'm meeting my boss for a makeover session that will create a whole new Gina."

That's what he was afraid of. "I like the old Gina."

"You're family, you have to say that." She headed for the door. "Trust me, not every man agrees with you. See you."

She was gone before he could respond.

Gage frowned. Something was wrong. He'd tried to stay connected to Gina during her years away, especially after the loss of their father. Asking her about it wouldn't do any good. Unlike the twins, she closely guarded her feelings and her high IQ further isolated her.

He was certain about one thing, though. Working in a bar wasn't the answer. Maybe he'd better have a talk with Max. Racy managed the staff, but the owner was an old friend of his dad's. He figured he could get Max to override Racy's hiring decision.

Confidence filled him as he went back to sorting his mail. The return address for the State Bar Association of Nevada on a business-size envelope caught his eye. A tightening in his gut told him it wasn't good news. The only dealing he'd had with Nevada lately was the annulment paperwork folded neatly in his top dresser-drawer. He opened the letter and started to read, not quite believing the words. Seconds later, he crushed the letter in his fist.

Racy was proud of herself. Gina had been in her company for over two hours and she still hadn't asked how her big brother had reacted to the news. She concentrated instead on getting to know Gage's sister and bringing out the beautiful girl hiding behind the baggy clothes and non-descript hairstyle.

Gina now sported contacts after she revealed she had them, but usually stuck with her glasses. He hair fell in a dark, smooth, glossy curtain and artfully applied makeup, a bit on the heavy side but perfect for the bar, played up those gorgeous Steele blue eyes.

When they'd arrived at The Blue Creek a few minutes ago, she'd given Gina a couple of T-shirts with the bar's logo to try on. The door to the ladies' restroom opened and Gina walked into the break room used by the rest of the staff.

"Hey, you look great."

"You don't think it's—" Gina tugged at the tee's cropped hem that rested above the low waistband of her new body-hugging jeans "—a bit too tight?"

"It's supposed to be tight, honey, and you have the body for it." Racy waved her over to the floor-length mirror. "See?"

The relief in the young girl's eyes when she saw her reflection pulled at Racy's heart. Not much surprised her anymore, but she'd been floored when the librarian look-alike had asked last night about a job. And she hadn't hired Gina purely for the satisfaction of getting to her older brother. No, she truly needed help, with two of her girls quitting a week ago.

Ruffling the sheriff's feathers was only an added bonus.

"We'll use the next few hours getting you used to the menu and the ordering system," she said. "You can practice carrying a trayful of drinks, too."

Gina nodded and they headed for the bar. A raucous country song blared over the sound system. A group of girls, lined up on the middle of the dance floor, broke out into precision dance steps. Horror crossed the girl's features. "I'm not going to be doing that, am I?"

Imagining the look on Gage's face when he found his sister dancing on the bar was priceless, but Racy wouldn't do that to Gina. Besides, Gage hadn't been back to The Blue Creek since the baseball play-offs melee.

Coward.

"No, those are the Blue Creek Belles. They didn't perform last night, but they dance as well as serve up food and drinks." Racy reached beneath the bar to lower the volume on the sound system. "I'm giving you the six tables in that area."

The relief on Gina's face switched to panic again. "Six? Are you sure?"

Racy grabbed menus and a large tray. "I'll be here if you need help, and the other girls will pitch in if things get busy."

"I really appreciate this." Gina leaned forward and propped her forearms on the bar. "I was going stir-crazy at home."

"It must be nice being back with your family."

Oh, real smooth. Try to get her to talk about her brother without coming right out and asking.

Gina leaned against the bar. "It is good to be home after being gone most of my life to private schools and then college. With Gage finally out of the house, I grabbed the converted attic, complete with its own bath."

Racy's hands stilled over the beer bottles in the under-counter cooler. "His place on the lake is done?"

Gina nodded, tucking a long strand of hair behind one ear. She opened the menu, studying the items intently. "Can you believe it? He's been working on that log house forever."

Four years, but who's counting? "Well, I'm sure he's happy to finally be in his own bachelor pad."

She had no idea how big of a place Gage had built, but she'd bet her entire Vegas winnings it came complete with an oversize hot tub, pool table and a king-size bed for all six-feet-plus of him.

The memory of another king-size bed, her body pressed deep into the cool sheets with Gage's hot, hard body draped over— Stop!

Racy groaned and yanked the bottles from the cooler. Doing nothing since Vegas but studying and working should've erased the memories of that crazy night, but no, they remained bright and strong and ever-present in her head.

"Hey, boss lady."

Racy looked up.

Ric Murphy, one of her security team members, stood behind Gina. "Max needs to see you in his office."

"Okay." She turned to Gina. "I'll be back in a minute."

"I'll be here."

Racy grinned and headed for the stairs that led to the second floor and her boss's office. Hopefully *her* office in a few months. A former musician, Max's band once had a couple of hits on country radio. He'd owned The Blue Creek since the early eighties and had joked about retiring ever since Racy had started working here. And after eight years of waitressing, then bartending and finally managing The Blue Creek, she was ready for the next step.

A step that had been only a dream until she had returned from Vegas with fifty grand in poker winnings.

And another ex-husband.

Her footsteps faltered on the top step. *No, not a husband. Ex or otherwise.* Her and Gage's twelve-hour marriage was a mistake, a lapse in judgment that she'd fixed and tried—erotic memories notwithstanding—to forget.

She stopped at the office door and knocked, waiting for Max's response. At the sound of his gruff bark, she entered and froze.

Dressed in jeans, cowboy boots and the same leather bomber jacket he'd worn for years, Gage Steele stood at the large window behind her boss's desk. He turned, leaned against the frame and stared straight at her. At least she thought so. The ivory Stetson he always wore was pulled low, shielding his eyes.

The Marlboro Man. In the flesh. Minus the cigarette, of course. Mr. Perfect wouldn't dare to do anything that might be considered a weakness.

"You wanted to see me?" Her tone was sharp, but Racy was glad she got the words past the sudden tightness of her throat.

What the hell was Gage doing here? Was it Gina?

That's stupid. Of course, he's here about his sister.

"Ah, there's a pair of scissors at the barbershop waiting on me." Max rose from behind his desk. He tugged a coat over his Western dress shirt. "I'll give you two some privacy."

"I thought you wanted to talk," Racy demanded.

Gage stayed silent as he moved out of the older man's way.

"Be nice." Max's words were low, his lips barely moving beneath his bushy gray mustache as he walked toward Racy. He grabbed the door to pull it closed behind him. "And don't make a mess of my office."

"Max—" He disappeared before Racy could say another word. She stared at the door for a long moment before the sound of a throat clearing had her whirling around.

"What do you want?"

Gage pushed away from the window. A deep breath expanded his shoulders. His open jacket revealed a dark red chambray shirt over a black thermal pullover. The undone buttons on both shirts showed off the strong column of his neck. Even in the dead of winter the man's skin carried a glow of deep bronze. A glow she remembered he had over every inch of his—

Racy mentally slammed the door shut on the memory. "Well?"

He shoved his hands into the pockets of his jacket and crossed the office to where she stood. "We need to talk."

His low voice caused a shiver to dance along her skin. She crossed her arms over her chest.

Dammit, the aged gray sweat jacket again.

Gage's sweat jacket. Normally, she never left her place with it on, but Gina had shown up while she was studying and she'd forgotten to take it off. She doubted he even remembered how she had come to own it, but she wasn't going to take that chance. Thankful for the tank top she wore underneath, a quick zip and the jacket was off her shoulders. She used the sleeves to tie it around her waist.

His eyes followed her every move. "Why'd you do that?"

Yeah, like she was going to tell him she was crazy enough to hold on to this thing all these years. "It's hot in here."

An unreadable emotion filled his blue eyes. He blinked and it was gone. But his gaze stayed on her as he moved forward until the toes of his boots grazed hers.

She didn't budge.

For the first time since that weekend in Vegas, she and Gage were alone. Something they'd managed to avoid all these months. Oh, they'd seen each other. It couldn't be helped in a town the size of Destiny, but they hadn't spoken.

Until now.

"What are you doing in my bar, Gage?"

The brim of his Stetson grazed her hair. "I thought this place belonged to Max."

Not for long. "On paper. I'm the one who keeps it running."

"Always to the point, aren't you?"

"What I am is busy." She broke free from his hypnotic gaze and again crossed her arms. A few side steps had her resting her backside against Max's desk. "So, why did you scare my boss out of his office?"

Gage turned, his clenched fists visibly pressing against the creased leather. "We need to talk about a couple of things—"

"And one of them is your sister." Racy cut him off with a wave of her hand. "You went to Max about her working here, and what? Called in an old family favor? But he told you to deal with me. So, go ahead. Give it your best shot."

"My best shot?"

"In convincing me to fire her, but I'll give you my answer right now. No way."

His mouth pressed into a hard line, then he said, "This is the last place Gina should be working."

She cocked her head to one side. "Because?"

"The girl has a master's degree in twentieth-century British and Irish studies."

"And that's going to hinder her in carrying a trayful of burgers and beer?"

"Dammit, Racy! She's not equipped to deal with the horny cowboys and college kids that come in here."

"Unlike me, you mean."

"You certainly have a way of keeping them in line."

From anyone else, she might've taken that as a compliment. Coming from Gage, it sounded more like an insult. "If you're referring to that brawl in October, I was handling everything just fine until you walked in."

"Including Dwayne. After I stopped his fist with my face."

She fought against a grin and lost. "You should've ducked." Her tone turned serious again. "Look, I wasn't going to let Dwayne use a lopsided loss by his team as an excuse to start a fight. Besides, his right hook didn't shake you up too bad."

"It hurt like hell."

Let it go. You don't want to go there. "Well, I'm sure the *ample* attention one of my Belles heaped on you led to a speedy recovery." *Too late, dammit!*

"Tammy brought me a raw steak for my eye."

"With a healthy side order of cleavage and fawning."

His gaze dropped from her face to her chest. Racy knew the flimsy cotton tank top was no match against the purple satin push-up bra filled with her own generous assets. She tightened her arms beneath her breasts and took a deep breath.

A single tic danced over his jaw. Served him right.

His gaze moved higher and lingered on her neck. She had to fight to keep her hand from going to her throat. The love bite he'd left above her collarbone was long gone. It had taken almost three weeks for the mark to disappear, but the memory of how she'd gotten it, and who'd given it to her, remained powerfully strong.

Especially when the man was standing right in front of her.

His eyes locked with hers again. "I think your Belles lead by your example."

"Your deputies must do the same. Tammy's got a busier social life than Britney Spears and Paris Hilton put together."

"Present company excluded. I'm not interested in Tammy."

He backed up a few steps and yanked off his hat. A quick push of his fingers through his dark hair left spiky tufts standing on end. They disappeared when he returned the Stetson to its proper place. "My point is Gina could be teaching at any college in the country."

"She's twenty-two years old." Racy broke in, glad he was backing off about the bar fight. And from her. She was still reeling from his statement about not being interested in her waitress. Why, she didn't want to consider. "Your sister wants to have some fun, meet people and wear sexy jeans."

"That's not Gina."

"Maybe you don't know her as well as you think." Racy

pushed away from the desk and took a wide circle around him. Not wide enough. Her bare arm brushed against his jacket as she headed for the door. The movement caused goose bumps to skate down to her fingers.

He followed. "We're not finished here."

"Yes, we are. I'm not firing Gina."

"This isn't about Gina. It's about us."

Racy's hand tightened on the doorknob as she wrenched it open. "Nice try in changing tactics, but there is no 'us.'"

"I'm talking about Vegas."

One booted foot hesitated at the threshold. A rocking country song that warned of T-R-O-U-B-L-E rang in the rafters. "We agreed to never bring that up again." She tossed the words over her shoulder.

Gage's arm shot out.

His palm landed against the doorjamb blocking her exit. "If you keep walking, I'm going to follow." He leaned in, his mouth at her ear in order to be heard over the loud music. "Do you want everyone to find out we're still married?"

Racy's vision blurred at his hotly whispered words. "What?"

Gage pulled her back into the office and kicked the door closed. He turned her to face him, the warmth of his touch on her bare shoulders searing her skin. He placed one hand beneath her chin and gently forced her to look him in the eye.

"Did you hear what I said?"

His rich baritone voice, barely above a whisper, caused a brand-new Vegas memory to spring to life. Five months ago he'd asked her the very same question. About what, she couldn't remember, but the recall left her feeling warm and fuzzy.

"Racy?"

She locked the memory away with the rest from that night and twisted free from his hold. "You're lying!"

"I'm—what? Why would I lie about something like this?"

She didn't know, but he had to be. How could they—no, they couldn't. They couldn't still be married! Two hours in that stuffy lawyer's office had taken care of the legal mumbo jumbo before they'd left Vegas. "If you're playing some sick game—"

A loud buzz cut off her words and brought forth a classic F-bomb she'd never heard Gage utter before. He grabbed the two-way radio from the belt clip at his hip and brought it to his mouth. "Steele here."

"Sheriff, Deputy Harris here."

His eyes never wavered from her. "What is it, Harris?"

Racy listened as the calm voice of one of her best friends filled the air. "We caught some kids drag racing on Razor Hill Road. Got one driver. Still in pursuit of the second."

"Fine, bring 'em in."

"Ah, Sheriff…Garrett is the driver."

His younger brother. Gage's eyes closed, but Racy still caught the shadow of fear in their blue depths.

"Was he—was anyone hurt?"

"Negative."

He released a held breath and opened his eyes. "Okay, I'll meet you at the office."

"Roger that. We're on our—wait one," a crackle came from the walkie-talkie before Leeann came back on. "Deputy Bailey just pulled up. He's got the second driver in custody."

"Good. Contact the parents of the other driver."

"Sheriff, the other driver is Giselle."

Racy bit back a choke of laughter, but part of it escaped in a loud *oomph*. Gage and Gina's twin siblings, both seniors at Destiny High School, caught drag racing. Each other.

Hell, she'd done the same thing many times as a teen in her father's rattrap of a pickup that hid a killer engine.

Usually against Bobby Winslow, who never seemed to get caught. But she had been, and her old man had left her overnight in jail while he and her brothers went on a bender in Cheyenne.

She doubted the Steele twins faced the same fate.

Gage's eyes narrowed as he took in her attempt to hold back her amusement. "I'm on my way. And take their cell phones. They aren't to talk to anyone until I get there."

"Their cell phones?" Racy asked.

Gage ended the call and jammed the radio back on his hip. "Those two will call our mother with a sob story so fast, she'll end up lecturing me instead of them."

Racy didn't doubt it. Sandy Steele was well known for her nurturing. Racy had experienced it firsthand years ago when the woman had provided a hot meal, a homemade quilt and a soft pillow to a scared teenage girl who'd spent the night in one of her husband's jail cells.

The heat of Gage's touch as he grabbed her hand and slapped an envelope into it yanked Racy back to the present.

"Read this," he said. "We'll talk later."

Her fingers curled around the letter as he headed for the door in Max's office that led directly to the front lobby. She read the envelope's return address. Her stomach dropped to her feet. "Gage, this…this can't be real."

"Oh, it's real." He paused at the door to look at her. "Welcome to my nightmare."

Racy stood frozen in place after he left. Then a knock came on the door. She shoved the envelope into her back pocket and turned. "Come in."

Gina peeked inside. "Has the smoke cleared?"

"What smoke?"

"No one can smolder better than my brother. Gage was here about me." The forlorn expression on Gina's face spoke volumes. "And don't ask me how I know. I'm the smart one, remember?"

Racy crossed the office and ushered the girl toward the stairs, quickly deciding it wasn't her place to relay the antics of Gina's younger siblings. She'd leave that for Gage or their mother. "Yes, he was here, and no, you aren't fired."

When Gina got to the bottom step she turned to face Racy. "The last thing you need is my big brother acting like…well, a big brother. Any more than he already does."

A pang Racy attributed to the craziness of what Gage had just told her hit her square in the gut. The folded envelope in her back pocket seemed to burn through her jeans.

"How's that?"

"You know, overprotective, watching my every move, staring down any guy that even looks at me."

So that's what big brothers did. Too bad nobody had filled in Billy Joe and Justin, who thought their sister was put on earth to keep their buddies occupied, steal bail money from and clean up after their lazy asses. Like father, like sons.

"Don't worry," Gina continued. "He'll behave tonight."

Racy focused on the young woman's assurance. "What?"

"He's here most nights."

"Gage hasn't been here in over two months."

"I was teasing him earlier—oh, that's right. He said he stays out of sight most of the time."

Out of sight? That's impossible.

Built on the same location as the original saloon, The Blue Creek had expanded over the years but remained on one level with an open floor plan. From her vantage point at the main bar, she could see everything, including the smaller bar on the far side near the pool tables and dartboards.

There were pockets of darkness, but there was no way Gage had stepped inside these walls and she hadn't known about it. The kitchen was off-limits to customers, as well as the second floor. The only rooms up there were Max's office and storage areas. Most of the doors off the balcony were fake, mimicking bedrooms where saloon girls would've taken—

The balcony.

Racy's gaze shot to the three-foot-wide area, complete with support beams and railing that ran three-quarters' way around the bar. Always in the shadows, but especially at night, someone could be there and she'd never know it.

How many nights had he done that? Before Vegas he used to come into the bar and deal with her face-to-face. Now he was hiding. And was that before or after he'd got the letter in her back pocket?

"Racy?" Gina's voice cut through her haze. "Are you okay?"

"I'm fine." Proud of the control in her voice, she pasted on a smile and showed Gina the easiest way to get a loaded tray off the bar without spilling its contents. "Why don't you practice carting this back and forth? It can get heavy."

Gina walked away and Racy again stared above her head. *Welcome to my nightmare.*

Gage's condescending words rang again in her ears. Okay. If he wanted to play games, she'd play. And if he wanted to watch, she'd give him a show to remember.

Chapter Three

Gage stepped from Max's office into the deafening noise, leaned against the wall and became one with the shadows. The Blue Creek was rocking with a live band, typical for a Saturday night. Bodies filled the dance floor and tempting smells wafted from the kitchen, causing his stomach to rumble. He'd missed dinner, thanks to spending most of the evening dealing with the twins and his mother.

Since their father's death ten years ago, his mother often took a soft road with his youngest sister and brother, resulting in him drawing a hard line when it came to their adolescent antics. Officially, they'd gotten off with a warning, but both were grounded for a month.

Damn, days like this he really missed his old man.

Gage had never got away with anything growing up. Then again, having your father as the town sheriff pretty much guaranteed you'd either be a rebel or a straight-up kid.

He'd been straight as an arrow. Not Garrett and Giselle.

First graders when their father was gunned down during a drug bust gone bad, they'd gone from good kids to trouble-makers in record time. He knew heartache was the driving force behind their behavior and their mother had been lost in her own grief-stricken haze. He'd returned from Washington, D.C., to make funeral arrangements, and moved back permanently a month later, leaving behind his dreams of working for the FBI, to take care of his family.

A family that at the moment was driving him crazy.

Not to mention that, at least legally, his family included Racy Dillon. As he'd often learned over the last ten years, sometimes life kicked you right in the ass.

His eyes followed Racy as she worked the main bar alongside two other bartenders, whose names didn't register in his brain. Nothing registered except for the trim, toned skin on display.

She had on something that looked like the top half of a bikini. Two scraps of dark material covered her breasts while below swayed a row of fringe that reached her navel and the glittery stone pierced there.

Except for the twin knots behind her neck and between her shoulder blades, her back was entirely exposed, thanks to her long red curls piled in a messy knot on top of her head. Low-rider jeans completed the look.

Gage dropped his head back against the wall and sighed. Ever since that crazy weekend in Vegas, his usually neat and orderly life had slowly slid out of control.

First Racy, and now Gina and the twins. Oh, and let's not forget his mother. When he'd finally reached her today, she'd been out at Hank Jarvis's place. Hanging curtains. A long-time family friend and widower for almost three decades, Hank worked at the Crescent Moon, Maggie Stevens's ranch.

Gage had been surprised as his mother's only interests since his dad died were the kids, and in the last couple of years, her job decorating cakes for the local inn. When asked, she'd insisted she and Hank were only friends. The pretty pink blush on her cheeks had told a different story.

He was yanked from his thoughts when Racy leaned across the bar, getting nose-to-nose with a customer. His stomach clenched. Good thing it was Willie Perkins, a local cowboy old enough to be his grandfather, or Gage would've—

Would've what?

So, she made him horny. Hell, she probably had that effect on every guy in the bar if their body parts worked properly.

But he knew what it was like to hold her in his arms.

Over the last five months, every exacting detail of their night together in Vegas had returned. He remembered the dusky scent of her skin, a mixture of vanilla and lime. The way her hands trembled when she touched him and the catch of her breath when his mouth found certain sensitive places on her body, like the small of her back, the inside of her elbow and the underside of her breasts.

Gage shifted his stance thanks to the pressure building behind his zipper. *Damn, he felt like a Peeping Tom up here.*

He'd returned to his rounds at The Blue Creek a little over a month ago. With Max's okay, he used his office as easy access to a spot that offered him a view of everything that went on in the bar. It also allowed him to watch his deputies to judge how they responded to any incidents.

And yeah, he could watch Racy.

She worked the back side of the bar, letting the other girls deal directly with the customers, easily handling three mixers and never missing a beat while popping the tops off ice-cold longnecks. She loaded them on a tray held by one of her waitresses. He didn't recognize her, but it didn't matter. He was only interested in keeping an eye on one other person and that was Gina. He scanned the crowd. Sexy waitress, sexy waitress, sexy wait—

Whoa, back up!

The waitress with the full tray turned. Gage registered her trim figure and long dark hair, but missing was the usual ponytail and glasses. That was no waitress. That was his sister.

"Wow, look at you!"

Racy felt more than heard the voice over her shoulder, thanks to the rocking country music. She turned and found her best friend, Maggie Stevens, soon to be Maggie Cartwright, standing behind her.

She shot a quick glance down at her outfit while moving to the end of the bar. "Yeah, look at me."

Maggie reached out, her fingers brushing at the fringe. "I love this! I'd never be able to pull it off, but on you…"

"Looks can be deceiving. I'm freezing my ass off."

"What's up with you behind the bar? You usually let the girls run the show."

"I'm trying to stay warm."

Confusion filled Maggie's eyes for a moment, then she smiled. "Where is he?"

"Where's who?"

"Oh, come on. Tell me you're not wearing that for a certain hunky sheriff."

Thankful when one of the bartenders called her name, Racy ducked back behind the three feet of wood. She tossed the requested bottle of whiskey to Jackie, confident her assistant manager would catch it. She took an extra minute to ensure her face was devoid of any expression before she turned back.

"What sheriff?"

Maggie leaned in. "Look, I know I've been distracted with the wedding—"

"And you have every right to be." Racy cut her off. "You waited a long time for the right man to come along. You deserve to be distracted…and happy."

"But that doesn't mean I don't have time to listen."

"To what?"

"You've been quiet—too quiet—about Gage since you two got back from Vegas."

"You sound like we were there together." It took all Racy's strength not to look up to the balcony. She knew he was there. Never mind the fact she hadn't seen him. "Besides, I told you we ran into each other a few times in the hotel. That's it."

"Uh-huh."

"Don't you have other things to worry about?" Racy latched on to the topic most likely to be on her best friend's mind, her upcoming wedding. "Like my bridesmaid's dress?"

Maggie smiled. "You haven't read your mail today?"

Racy shook her head. The only letter she'd had time to read today was the one Gage had given her. A lot of legal double-talk that came to the same conclusion.

She and the sheriff were still legally man and wife.

The date on the notice was over two weeks old. She'd fumed that he'd known about this mess for that long and only told her today, *after* he'd found out about his sister taking a job here.

"No, I was working with a new waitress and one emergency after another happened in the kitchen this afternoon."

"I put a note in your wedding invitation. The dresses are all set except for the final fitting. You're going to knock him for a loop when he sees you."

"Knock who?"

Maggie grinned then said, "Of course, it doesn't quite have the flair of this outfit. I think something's brewing—"

"The only thing brewing is a wicked headache," Racy paused when the band announced it was taking a break. She hit the switch on the bar's stereo system and recorded music filled the air. "And a good case of frostbite."

"Okay, I give up. You got any plans for tomorrow?"

Racy shook her head. "Nope. What's up?"

"How about getting with Leeann for lunch around noon?"

"Are you sure the good deputy is going to show? She's blown us off more times than I can count."

Maggie nodded and Racy read worry in her gaze over their best friend. "She's the one who suggested it. Did you know whoever bought her family's land last year finally tore down the remains of the house?"

"There wasn't much left after the fire."

"And still Leeann held on to it. I think selling was the best thing she's done in a long time. But to know someone is building there again…"

Racy frowned as Maggie's voice faded. Their friend's childhood home, an antebellum-style mansion, was situated on the side of a mountain surrounded by acres of land. When a fire had destroyed the house five years ago, many had been surprised Leeann didn't sell outright, or rebuild when she'd finally moved back to town.

"Maybe the corporation that bought it is going to make it into some kind of resort. Anyway, count me in." Racy noticed the arrival of Maggie's fiancé, Landon Cartwright, as he strolled through the archway leading from the main entrance. "Hey, your honey just walked in. Who's the cowboy with him?"

Pure joy filled Maggie's expression before she looked over her shoulder. Racy was happy for her friend. If anyone deserved to be loved by a good man it was Maggie.

"That's Chase, my future brother-in-law." Maggie turned back. "He's here for the wedding."

Racy took in the man's tall frame and wide shoulders. He was a few inches shorter than Landon, but shared the same sharp facial features and dark skin, even in the dead of winter. He filled out his cotton shirt and jeans nicely, drawing more than a few feminine glances his way.

She waited for the zing of attraction. Nothing. Why was it no man stole the air from her lungs? Or made all the interesting parts of her body turn to mush?

Nowadays, only one man made her feel anything, and at the moment it was pure loathing. And to get back at that man, Chase Cartwright would be perfect for what she had in mind.

"Do you think he'd be up for a little fun?"

"Why? What are you planning?"

She nodded toward the bar. "I think it's time for another Racy Special."

"Are you serious? You haven't done one in months after that last guy—ewww! That was not fun to watch."

"I swore that one was going to be my last, but something's come up—anyway, my tip jar is getting low." Racy slipped a folded bill into Maggie's hand. "Here, give this to your brother-in-law and explain how it works, okay? I don't want to take his money."

"Why do I get the feeling this has to do with Gage?"

"Because you're too smart for your own good." Racy grinned. "Go on, your family's waiting. And be nice to your waitress. She's new."

Maggie eyed the young girl at their table. "She looks familiar."

"That's Gina Steele." Racy grabbed the microphone from behind the bar.

"Gage's sister? The whiz kid?"

"That's her."

"First his sister—" Maggie waved at the bar "—and now this? I thought you said Gage hasn't been in here in a while."

"I said I haven't *seen* him here."

"There's a difference?"

"Yes."

"You know, I'm going to ply you with margaritas at my bachelorette party to get the whole scoop on this," Maggie whispered, then turned and headed for her fiancé.

Yeah, like she was going to spill how too much booze and an old dream had caused her to make the biggest mistake of her life.

Racy locked down any Vegas memories before they could surface. A trick she was getting pretty good at lately.

She brushed a hand against the trophy, a physical reminder of what really mattered. A quick yank on a few well-placed bobby pins, and her hair fell past her shoulders. She whispered her plans to her fellow bartender and, thanks to a step stool and the vertical cooler, stood on the L-shaped bar.

A piercing whistle got everyone's attention. She rarely got up here anymore, preferring to stick to choreographing the Belles' dance routines.

Tonight was different. With her back to the balcony, she couldn't see the man who technically had been her husband for the last five months, but her skin tingled.

He was watching.

"Welcome to The Blue Creek!" She addressed the crowd and they cheered. "It might be cold and snowy outside, but it's hot in here. And while the band is taking a well-earned break, I think it's time we raise the heat!"

Ignoring the surprised looks from her waitresses, Racy waved to the girls who made up the dance team. The cheers from the crowd grew when they joined her on the bar. "It's time for a down-home boot stomping!"

The music started and Racy fell into the familiar steps. She dipped and stomped and grabbed Willie's tattered straw cowboy hat, plopping it right on her head.

Exaggerating the curve of her hips, she turned to face the shadowed balcony, the hat low over her eyes to conceal the direction of her stare. The short end of the bar was hers alone and she made good use of the space.

Sweat beaded on her forehead as she pictured Gage's blue eyes turning a stormy indigo like they did when he got angry. Or turned on. It was part of the ever-growing collection of memories that continued to haunt her.

One of her favorites was the two of them on the dance floor. Their bodies so close she felt the outline of every hard muscle. His hands clenched her hips as she moved against him, never breaking eye contact. Song after song, until he pulled her off the dance floor and into a dark alcove. The width of his shoulders blocked the outside world, the wide brim of his Stetson created a private canopy as he pressed her against the wall with a kiss that stole her breath.

The music ended and the bar erupted in thunderous applause. Racy bowed, and blamed the wild beating of her heart on the dancing as she handed Willie back his hat.

"Let's hear it for the Blue Creek Belles!" She huffed into the microphone, pushing the words past her dry throat.

One down. One to go.

"Ya'll enjoy that?" She was rewarded with cheers while her girls got down from the bar. "I bet ya'll have worked up a mighty thirst. I know I did."

She motioned to Jackie, who recognized the hand signal. Seconds later, a shot glass filled with a golden liquid was handed to her. To the crowd it was tequila. To Racy it was ice-cold apple juice and not nearly enough to quench her thirst.

She tossed it back, took a deep breath and, for a moment, questioned if she was doing the right thing.

But she couldn't back out now.

Gage knew what was coming.

Hell, he was still trying to recover from her dancing.

Every bump and grind of her hips brought back to life the hours he'd spent with her. The same red waves he'd buried his face in flew over her shoulders and skimmed across her naked back. The dark blue fringe of her top brushed against the toned stomach he'd covered in a trail of wet kisses.

It had been years since she'd danced with the girls, but she still had the moves. Moves he was intimately familiar with. It wasn't until the music stopped that he managed to get his breathing under control. Now she was going to—

Racy held up the empty glass. "Anyone else want one?"

She laughed when the crowd shouted in agreement and surged forward. Gage immediately sought out his sister. Relief filled his chest when he found her against the back wall with another waitress and one of the bouncers.

"I'll take that as a yes." Racy's singsong voice called out over the crowd, pulling Gage's attention back to her. "Seeing how my tip jar is getting low, I think we need a special…."

The regulars in the crowd knew what was coming and roared their approval.

Damn, it was getting warm in here. Gage yanked down the zipper of his bomber jacket, desire tightening his chest.

"Now, what I need is a very thirsty cowboy, but not just any cowboy." I need someone with all the right moves…who is willing to part with his money!" Racy held aloft the empty shot glass. "The going rate for a Racy Special is one hundred dollars. Do I have any takers?"

Despite the absurd price, there were plenty of men willing to part with their cash. When word spread just what a Racy Special included, even more hands shot into the air.

He couldn't believe she was still pulling this stunt.

"So many choices." Racy dropped her voice to a throaty rumble. "The tall, dark and handsome stranger in the back." She waved at a man who moved through the crowd toward the bar. Gage zeroed in on him, noting he was everything Racy said. "You got the cash, honey?"

The man smiled and held up a hundred-dollar bill between two fingers. Gage caught something familiar in his face. Did he know this guy?

"What's your name, sugar?" Racy asked, taking the money and making a show of tucking it into the deep V of her top.

"Chase." The man's deep voice carried over the microphone.

"You're not one of our locals, Chase," Racy said. "Don't tell me you're a University of Wyoming Cowboy?"

Racy's question brought more cheers as the band broke into "Ragtime Cowboy Joe," the university fight song. The University of Wyoming in Laramie was less than an hour's drive south, and The Blue Creek was a favorite among the college crowd.

"It's a few years since my college days," the man said when Racy stuck the microphone under his nose again. "I'm from Texas."

"Oh, Texas…love that Southern drawl."

Gage thought he was going to puke.

"Okay, let's give a paying customer some room." Racy waved away the bar patrons, who moved back into the crowd, taking their drinks with them. She traded her empty shot glass for one filled to the brim, then slowly turned to face the cowboy.

"That's it?" he asked, looking up at her on the bar.

"Oh, no, I'm not done with you yet."

Gage's gut tightened into a painful knot.

Racy backed up and crooked her finger, motioning the cowboy to join her. He grinned and easily climbed up on the scarred wood surface.

From this angle, Gage couldn't see the man's expression, but he could imagine what he was thinking with almost six feet of toned, sexy female standing right there in front of him.

"Now, sweeties, you hold on to me while I hold on to this," Racy said, before handing off the microphone and raising the shot glass over her head.

Gage's hands curled into fists as the crowd roared its approval when the music started again.

Racy once again put her arsenal of bumps and grinds to good use as the cowboy took her in his arms in a modified two-step. She didn't spill a drop while they moved in a timeless rhythm that would've been blatantly sexual if they'd been horizontal.

A hot jolt of something he refused to label raced through Gage's veins as he watched. A rush of pent-up air escaped his lips when the music finally ended and the crowd applauded.

Racy spoke but he couldn't hear her words as the cheering grew louder when the cowboy nodded. She motioned to the bar where a saltshaker and wedge of lime sat on a small tray. With one hand on his shoulder, she directed the cowboy to his knees.

"Now, a Racy S-special isn't just a s-shot of Mexican blue agave tequila *reposado*."

Her voice shook as she spoke, the crowd now hushed. "To do this properly you need the right inducements."

Gage mentally nailed his boots to the floor. It took every ounce of his willpower not to march downstairs and yank her ass off the bar. What the hell was she trying to prove? Hadn't she learned—

Wait, did she just look up at him?

She pulled in a deep breath, her voice strong again as she swung her long curls off the face with a practiced toss of her head. "Let me demonstrate. The rest of you are welcome to watch so you can try this in the privacy of your own home."

Taking the saltshaker from the cowboy's outstretched hand, she raised her left wrist to her mouth. Gage could've sworn she was staring right at him as her tongue left a damp path on her skin. She then held the arm and sprinkled salt over the area.

Moving closer, she balanced her salt-encrusted arm on his shoulder and held the shot glass inches from his mouth. Piercing whistles and catcalls raced through the crowd.

"Don't make me laugh, ya'll, can't spill good booze." Racy addressed the crowd before turning her attention back to the cowboy. "Okay, sugar. You're welcome to take your shot whenever you're ready."

Again, her gaze lifted to her overhead lights. No, that wasn't right. She was staring up at the balcony. At him.

The cowboy remained still for a long moment. Then he rose, ignoring her salt-covered skin and tossing the lime over his shoulder. Leaning forward, he captured the shot glass with his mouth, tipped his head back and downed the booze in one swallow before releasing the glass into his hand.

The crowd cheered and the band went live with a rocking country song when the cowboy lifted Racy's hand to his mouth and kissed it before jumping back to the floor.

Gage found himself torn between respect for the guy and the urge to tear the man's heart out of his chest.

Lucky bastard.

Racy tried to concentrate on the computer screen. Chase Cartwright's words, whispered before he'd jumped off the bar, still rang in her ears. At first, she'd had no idea what he was talking about. Then he'd winked and said if she needed any help making her guy jealous, he'd be in town for a couple of weeks.

Her guy? Yeah, right.

She'd mumbled thanks and spent the rest of the night trying to justify to herself why she'd done it. Had it been worth it? She wasn't sure Gage had seen her performance.

Keeping an eye out for him the rest of the night had produced nothing. If he was in the bar, he'd managed to stay hidden.

Until closing time.

She and Max had decided to close up an hour early due to a surprise snowstorm predicted to accumulate several inches. After the staff had cleaned up, Gina had given her a hug goodbye. Racy had quickly picked up that she was upset.

When she had pressed, thinking it was job related, Gina had said her jailer was waiting to take her home. Powerless not to, she'd looked and found Gage's hard stare directed at her.

Too far away to see his eyes, his clenched jaw and his arms folded over his chest told her either he'd indeed witnessed her entire act or he was still pissed about his sister working here.

His gaze had held hers until Gina had walked past and slugged him in the arm. Then they both had disappeared out the door.

"I'm heading out, sweetheart. You ready to go?"

Racy looked up and found Max in the doorway. "I need to finish this paperwork."

"I had planned to head home long ago." The man's grin rose into his mustache. "Look what I would've missed."

She took a swallow of ginger ale from a nearby glass. "Give me a break. I haven't done that in months."

Max yanked on his gloves. "Which makes me wonder, what's got you so riled that you'd do it again? Not to mention shaking your butt on the bar."

Racy broke free of her boss's speculative gaze and turned back to the computer's bookkeeping program. "Just wanted to see if I could still keep up."

"You kicked ass and you know it. Don't be long, ya hear?

It's a winter wonderland out there." He sighed. "All this white stuff makes me long for the warmth of the South."

A fact Racy was counting on when she presented her proposal to buy him out. "Another fifteen minutes, I promise."

She concentrated on her work, pausing a few minutes later to push at the sleeve on her oversize sweatshirt. One with the bar's logo, not Gage's sweat jacket. That was buried in her backpack. And as soon as she got home it was going to the bottom of her closet.

A quick glance at her watch told her it was almost 2:00 a.m. Wow, she hadn't known it was that late. Crashing on the battered leather couch against the far wall wasn't an option. No, she had to go home because—

A muffled, steady clapping caused Racy to jump.

She swung around. Gage. He leaned against the door frame, his Stetson and jacket stained from wet snow. Cheeks ruddy from the cold, his lips pressed in a hard line as he continued a measured applause.

"Cut it out. You scared the crap out of me." Was she as breathless as she sounded? "How did you get—ah, Max. Look, I know Gina working here has you twisted six ways from Sunday, but I've already told you she's staying."

He'd stopped clapping and shoved his hands into his jacket pockets. "She told me the same thing on the ride home. I was heading to my place when I saw your car in the parking lot. Come on, I'll give you a lift."

"Excuse me?"

"You don't have snow tires. I checked. Got chains in the trunk?"

She didn't speak, knowing her silence gave him his answer.

"That's what I figured." He entered her office. "Besides, you've been drinking."

Racy glanced at the glass. "That's only—"

"I don't care what it is. Mixed with the shot you had earlier, it's two drinks too many."

She frowned in confusion until she realized he was talking about the shot glass of apple juice.

Hmm, so he had seen everything. She should be happy, but deep inside she wondered if it mattered. He probably wouldn't give two whiffs if she'd stripped down to nothing and got it on with the first cowboy to cross her path.

Of course, the last cowboy she'd gotten skin-to-skin with was standing right in front of her.

"Oh, please, like you're worried about me." She turned back to the monitor, but fatigue overcame her. It was time to go home. In her own car. Three clicks and the computer started its shutdown. "I'm exhausted."

"That's understandable." He spun her toward him.

She gasped, never hearing him cross the room. He leaned in, his hands gripping the chair's wood handles, trapping her. "Considering the workout you got tonight."

Her eyes slammed into his. She tried to back up, but there was nowhere to go. The man surrounded her. The clean, fresh scent of snow and the outdoors clung to his clothes. It mixed with the warm, earthy scent of his skin to swirl around her, but she forced herself not to look away.

It was like being back in high school all over again!

He tugged on the chair, inching it closer. "Most husbands wouldn't enjoy seeing their wives parade on a bar in front of a bunch of drunk, horny cowboys."

"I don't have a husband."

His head dipped lower and thick lashes fanned out over sharp cheekbones as his gaze dropped to her mouth. He spoke, his voice barely a whisper as his eyes rose again to lock with hers. "We're still married. And, Mrs. Steele, we need to talk."

Chapter Four

*M*rs. Steele. Mrs. Steele. Mrs. Steele.

The words churned inside Racy's head much like the heavy snow swirling in the bright glow of the Jeep's headlights. She stared out into the darkness, not remembering exactly how she'd made it into Gage's vehicle. Her purse and backpack were at her feet, and on her lap were the matching letters from the State Bar of Nevada, one addressed to her and one to Gage.

That much she did remember. Clawing through the stack of mail on her desk to find her own letter explaining the legal mess they were in. A part of her had wanted to believe the letter Gage had given her was an elaborate joke. It wasn't.

"You're too damn quiet over there."

His harsh words caused her stomach to clench. She closed her eyes and kept her face toward the window. "I'm fine."

"All things considered."

"All things considered," she echoed softly.

"You're taking this better than I thought you would."

"Give me a few minutes. I'll turn into the spitting hellcat you're used to."

"I'm waiting with bated breath."

Gage's tone was low, unforgiving. She turned to face him. His rugged profile was lost in the shadows, but the glow of the dashboard accented the hard line of his jaw. Her fingers tightened on the letters.

"Of all the lawyers in Vegas—"

"Leave it to us to find the worst one in town."

"Are you sure this is for real?" Racy waved the letters at him. If he wasn't playing a joke, maybe someone else was. "How do we know someone isn't messing with us?"

"Who else knows we let booze and the bright lights of Sin City lead us down the aisle? I haven't told anyone."

His words caused a sharp zinger to nail her in the chest. "Like I have?"

"I don't know. You ladies love to talk."

Not about this.

Despite the teasing threat issued earlier, Racy hadn't been tempted to confide in Maggie about what had happened between her and Gage. She knew her best friend—in the midst of her own romance-induced haze, thanks to falling for the cowboy she'd hired last summer—would turn a crazy night in Vegas into a bigger deal than the mere mistake it was.

And in a town the size of Destiny, it wouldn't take long for everyone else to find out. She couldn't take that. It was hard enough to live down her first two miserable marriages. Once it got out she'd been the one who'd done the actual proposing, everyone would think Gage had married her out of pity.

Or as a joke.

Why else would the town's hero hook up with her?

No, dealing with the local gossip chain was the last thing she needed while trying to put together her buyout plan for The Blue Creek.

So pulling a Racy Special wasn't the smartest move, huh?

Racy pushed away the thought, despite the twinge of satisfaction that filled her. Getting her rebellious side to cooperate with the businesswoman she wanted to be wasn't easy. At least she'd used her brain and deposited her Vegas winnings in a bank down in Laramie.

Could that be it? Was this screwup somehow connected to her winnings? "Did you tell anyone about the money I scored—"

"No. How would I explain I knew you're a card shark?"

"I'm not a shark." On a whim she'd used her bartenders challenge winnings to stake a claim in a no-holds-barred Texas hold 'em game. It would've been foolish if she hadn't won. And won big. "I was lucky."

"Yeah, that's us…lucky."

Gage took the turnoff to her house, and the Jeep slid across the unplowed road. He tightened his grip on the steering wheel, easily controlling the oversize vehicle. "Damn, these roads are bad. I can't believe you thought you could drive home. You should've used some of those winnings to buy yourself a decent car."

Not a chance. She had other plans for that money. She took a deep breath to calm her nerves but only succeeded in drawing in the clean, woodsy scent of the man next to her. Something she'd been trying to avoid since he'd shown up in her office, but hell, she needed air.

"I like my car and I have snow tires. I just haven't put them on yet."

"I'd ask why, but I'd bet you'd tell me to mind my own business."

Damn straight. "Wouldn't even give you odds."

"Lady, I've learned never to gamble when it comes to you."

"Afraid you'll come out on the losing end?"

His stare cut to her for a quick moment. "I think I accomplished that in Vegas."

Ouch, direct hit. Racy turned back to the window. "Just shut up and get me home."

There was nothing they could do about this marriage mess tonight and Gage was in no mood to talk rationally. The anger rolled off him in waves. Was it finding out they were still legally bound to each other? Or was it something else?

The Jeep slowly crawled along the snow-covered road that made up her long driveway. Her place was the only one out here. Her father and brothers had preferred it that way. No one around to complain about their extracurricular activities.

Living here by herself for the last seven years, not counting her brief second marriage, Racy enjoyed the solitude even if she never had the money to fix up the simple ranch house. Husband number two had seen to that when he'd run out with the entire contents of her bank account. *Jerk.*

"I know people leave a light on, but isn't this a bit much?"

Gage's words pulled Racy from her thoughts. As they rounded the last turn, she saw bright lights shining from every window. They stopped in front of the sagging covered porch that ran the length of the house. Deafening rock music drowned the soft country tunes coming from the Jeep's stereo. Two snow-covered cars sat askew in the front yard.

"You have guests?" Gage put the vehicle into park, but left it running.

She shook her head. "I don't know what's going on."

Gage grabbed his Stetson. "Stay here."

A tall figure opened the front door and staggered onto the porch. Racy gasped. Her stomach plummeted to her feet as she recognized the man, who looked right at home with a beer in one hand and a cigar in the other.

"Gage." She grabbed one leather-clad arm and nodded toward the house. "Wait."

He looked, then his gaze shot back to her. "Did you know about this?"

Racy opened her mouth, but nothing came out.

"Are you trying to tell me—ah, the hell with it." He yanked away from her touch and opened the Jeep's door.

She did the same. Her feet sank into the snow as she hurried past the still shining headlights. Gage was already up the steps by the time she joined him.

"Well, if it isn't the honorable sheriff of Destiny. Are you the welcome wagon, too?" The man fell against the porch post and belched. "Hey, sis. You're out of bacon and eggs."

Racy closed her eyes, offered a quick prayer this wasn't happening and opened them again. No, he was still here. Billy Joe, her eldest brother by five years and until very recently a resident of the Wyoming prison system.

"What are you doing here?"

"Well, that's a fine howdy-do." Billy Joe straightened and started toward her. "I expected better from family. Come 'ere and give your big brother a kiss."

Gage instantly moved between them. All Racy saw was the wide span of his shoulders. "That's far enough, Dillon." His voice was easily heard over the loud music. "I think Racy asked you a question. I'll repeat it. What are you doing here?"

"I live here."

No, he doesn't!

Racy bit hard at her bottom lip, stopping her outcry. Thanks to a small insurance policy from her first husband, she'd bought out her brothers years ago. She had no idea they'd used the money to set up a drug-running business. A business that had landed them behind bars eighteen months later.

But Billy Joe was out now, nearly two years earlier than their scheduled release date.

"Where's Justin?" She stepped around Gage, but noticed how he angled his body so he still stood between her and her brother. "Is he here with you?"

Billy waved a hand at the front door. "Inside, entertaining our guests." He took a long draw on the beer before tossing the can into the snow. "The Dillon boys are out, Sheriff Steele. Wanna see our paperwork?"

"Yes."

Her brother headed for the front door with Racy right behind him. Before she could go more than a few steps, Gage seized her wrist. "You really didn't know they were back in town?"

She whipped back around. His icy-blue eyes stared at her. Was that disbelief she read in their cool depths? "I'm as surprised as you."

"They've been here awhile. The question is how long."

"How do you know that?"

"There weren't any tracks on the road, and those cars—" he jerked his thumb over his shoulder "—are covered with at least four inches of snow."

"I haven't seen or talked to either of my brothers in over two years." She yanked her hand free. "I told you, I don't know what's going on."

She turned, unwilling to see the disapproval on his face. He muttered under his breath as he followed, but she couldn't make out the words. Good thing, too. He was probably damning the entire Dillon family to hell.

The moment she stepped into her living room, she froze. Gage bumped into her, grabbing her upper arms and she found herself leaning into his strength. The furniture had been around since Racy's childhood. The end tables, lamps and television cabinet were yard-sale finds. Former sheets made up the curtains and long-ago-pilfered milk crates lined one wall as bookcases. It'd never be on the cover of a home decorating magazine, but it had always been clean and in order.

Until tonight.

Empty pizza boxes and beer bottles littered the tables and floor. Her paperbacks lay scattered, as if they had been thrown against the wall and then left where they'd dropped. Her college textbooks made a makeshift table for an open case of beer, and a fifth of whiskey lay tipped over, its contents creating a dark puddle in the aged shag carpet. The living room opened into the kitchen, which looked like a disaster zone with dishes and pans covering every inch of counter space. A pungent odor of beer, burnt eggs and smoke filled her nose.

"Hey, sis!" Justin Dillon sat on the couch, his arms around two blondes who looked like they came straight from a city street corner. "Aren't ya glad to see us?"

Racy slumped. He was drunk. They both were and her home was trashed. Embarrassment heated her face. The tightening of Gage's hands on her shoulders, in sympathy or anger, only made it worse. She pulled in a deep breath and wrenched from his grasp.

"I think she's mad," Justin said, grinning like a loon. "Sorry for the mess. Don't worry, we'll clean it up."

"Like hell we will. That's what she's here for." Billy strolled back into the room and hit the power button on the old stereo, cutting off the noise. He shoved the paperwork at Gage. "It's all legal. There ain't nothing you can do about it."

Racy ignored her brothers and walked farther into the room. She couldn't believe the damage they'd done in a matter of hours. She and Gina had left—

Gina! Her stomached clenched. Oh, thank God she hadn't been here when they'd shown up. But someone had been. Someone who'd waited for her every night for the last couple of months.

"Ohmigod, what have you done with Jack?"

The panic in Racy's voice made Gage look up.

"Where is he? I swear if you've done something—" Racy ran into the kitchen and headed for the back door. She yanked it open and yelled into the night. "Jack! Jack, come here, boy!"

The clicking of nails on the floor came from what Gage guessed was a back hallway. He'd never been farther inside the Dillon house than the living room. Not even nine years ago when he'd come to tell them about the deaths of their father and Racy's husband.

He still remembered that night.

The loss of his own father the summer before had been a fresh, pain-filled memory when he'd driven here after finding no one at the shabby apartment where she'd lived in town. He'd stood on the front porch and tried to keep his eyes off the long, sexy legs of another man's widow as he'd delivered the news.

Racy cried out, bringing him back to the present. She dropped to her knees as the golden retriever staggered into the kitchen. The animal wagged its tail when it caught sight of her, then sprawled to the floor, his legs giving way.

"Oh, Jack!"

The fear in Racy's voice created a hard press of empathy and anger in Gage's chest. She crawled across the linoleum to the dog and cradled its head in her lap.

"What have you done?" Her eyes were hard as she focused on Billy Joe.

"Relax." Billy Joe spoke around the cigar he shoved between his teeth. "He just wanted to join the celebration. All that barking when we arrived got him a bit thirsty."

"You gave him alcohol?"

"You broke in here?" Gage's question overlapped Racy's. He handed the paperwork back to Billy Joe. "Breaking and entering is a good way to make these null and void."

"Y-you're crazy, Steele," Billy Joe sputtered. "W-we live here."

"You haven't lived here for years and if your sister changed the locks, then you two—" his stare took in Justin, who'd risen from the couch "—are once again breaking the law."

"Tell lover-boy this is our home, too," Billy Joe directed his sister.

Gage clenched his jaw, not allowing a reaction to Billy's comment. He looked at Racy and found her staring at him, face pale.

Her gaze flickered to her brother. "Shut up, Billy."

"What's the matter with you, girl? You've gone soft on the sheriff?" Billy Joe grunted. "Back when he was nothing but a snot-nosed football star you used to call him a dumb jock."

"He's not my lover." She swallowed hard and looked away, her attention on the dog. Her words came out in a ragged whisper. "I'm the only family Billy Joe and Justin have in this town and they're obviously in no shape to drive. They can stay here."

Gage ignored the pang in his chest. He concentrated instead on the fact she was letting the bastards off the hook. "Racy, you don't have to—"

"To worry about that mutt of yours," Billy Joe cut off Gage's protest and grabbed another beer. "We didn't let him have any of the good stuff. A few brewskis ain't going to kill him."

"Shut your trap, Billy." Racy continued to rub the dog's golden-brown fur. "Before I change my mind and you two can sleep it off in a jail cell."

A retching bellow from the retriever had Racy and the blonde girls on the couch crying out as the dog flopped into unconsciousness.

"Jack!" She grabbed a dish towel off a kitchen chair and wiped at the dog. "Oh, please wake up!"

Gage pushed past Racy's laughing jerk of a brother and reached her side in seconds. "Get a blanket."

She turned to him, her dark brown eyes filled with unshed tears. His anger at her…over Gina…their marriage…faded at the hurting in her gaze. He found himself wanting to pull her into his arms.

Instead, he pushed her to her feet and turned her toward the hallway. "Now."

She nodded and raced to a back room. Gage, mindful of the mess, stepped over the dog, keeping his eye on both of Racy's brothers. "Since neither one of you seems to be in a mood to help, why don't you sit back down with your…guests?"

"I'll help." Justin took a couple of unsteady steps. "What do you need?"

"Shut up and sit down." Billy Joe shoved Justin back toward the couch and the bewildered blondes. He turned and grinned at Gage. "Want us where you can see us, huh?"

"Yeah, something like that."

Gage knelt when Racy rushed back in with an oversize quilt. He hated to lose the use of his hands but he guessed the animal weighed at least seventy pounds. There was no way she'd be able to pick him up. He gathered the dog in his arms. They had to get help and fast.

Keeping an eye on Billy Joe, lounging in a battered recliner, and Justin, who sat nearby bug-eyed and white as a sheet, Gage pushed to his feet. "Racy, get the door."

She ran ahead and Gage followed. He held the dog much like he would a baby, with most of the weight on one arm just in case he needed to reach for his gun. It wouldn't be easy, but he'd do it if one of the Dillon boys rushed them.

He hated to leave them here, but they had to get the animal to the vet immediately. He made a mental note to call in a drive-by for one of his deputies as soon as he could. "Close the inside door," he said once they were on the porch. "Then get in the backseat."

Racy did what she was told. The rock music blared to life again as he hurried down the steps in an awkward backward motion. The urge to bust up their little party burned in his gut, but he knew there'd be plenty of other chances.

He slid the dog onto the backseat next to Racy, ordered her to put her seat belt on and then jumped in the driver's seat. The snow had slowed a bit, but the winds had picked up. He put the Jeep into gear and headed back the way they'd come.

He grabbed his cell phone from his pocket and pressed speed dial. "Hey, Kali…it's Gage," he said, when the veterinarian at the other end offered a sleepy hello. "Sorry to wake you, but I've got an emergency. I'm on my way to your place with a golden retriever, age…"

"Eight months," Racy whispered from the backseat.

"Eight months," he repeated, "that's been fed alcohol, beer most likely. Don't know how much or even how long ago. He got sick and passed out just a few moments ago."

"Tell her it's Jack. I had him in for a checkup last week."

Gage relayed the information and promised to get to her clinic as soon as he could. Ending the call, he pulled out onto the main road, glad to see the snowplows and salt trucks had made a pass on this stretch of highway.

He looked in his rearview mirror, but all he saw was snow-covered windows. A quick glance over his shoulder found Racy bent at the waist, caressing the dog's matted coat and murmuring softly to him, much like a mother would do to a sick child.

Gage focused back on the road. "Kali said it didn't hurt the dog to get sick. I'm guessing it cleared out his stomach."

"But he's not waking up and the alcohol is still swimming in his system," Racy said. "God only knows how much they gave him."

"When did you head to work this afternoon?"

"Gina and I left around four."

Gage tightened his grip on the steering wheel, his knuckles turning white. His anger flared to life again. He glared into the mirror. "Just how long have those bastards been around?"

Racy's head shot up. Her eyes were lost in the shadows, but he could see the hard line of her mouth. "Those bastards are my brothers. And they must've showed up after we left."

"And broke into your house."

She raised her chin. "I left the place unlocked."

Gage believed her claim about not knowing her brothers had been released—her response had been too genuine. But instinct told him she was covering for them now. What he didn't understand was why.

Her lie sat like a rock in his gut. Maybe because one of the things he'd always admired about Racy was her honesty. She never held back the truth about anything. Even when she'd told him their amazing night in Vegas had been a mistake.

He eyed the digital readout from the dashboard clock.

2:33 a.m. Five months ago today, to the minute, he'd actually married this woman. Happy freaking anniversary.

For richer or for poorer…
Whose fingers were trembling? Hers or his? He winked and squeezed her hand. Okay, they were hers.
In good times and bad…

What bad times? It had been all good...all night long. And they hadn't even gotten to the suite yet. She hoped it had a hot tub.

To love and to cherish...

Oh, no, getting teary eyed. Concentrate on Preacher Elvis's sequined bell-bottoms.

From this day forward until death do us part...

His job was dangerous. He always carried a weapon. He had one on him right now. She'd felt it pressed against her when he'd pulled her into a deep kiss during the taxi ride here. Not that Destiny was a thriving hotbed of crime, her family not included. Still, his father had died in the line of duty.

I now pronounce you man and wife...

"Racy."

He whispered her name as he lowered his head.

"Racy."

He said it again just before his lips swept over hers—

"Hey, Sleeping Beauty. Wake up."

Racy's eyes flew open. A wave of cold air smacked her in the face. She jerked upright in her seat and pushed her hair out of her eyes.

Oh, yuck. Her heart clenched. Jack.

She and her beautiful golden had found each other just after she'd returned from Vegas. He was the most sweet and loyal male in her life ever. Now he was at the vet clinic with an IV, being kept for observation.

Kali Watson had reassured her Jack would be okay, but she wanted to monitor him overnight, even after he'd finally awakened. Racy had nodded in agreement and every last ounce of her energy had departed. She climbed into the front seat of Gage's Jeep, and promptly fell asleep, dreaming about the moment she and Gage had become man and wife.

Another gust of wind washed over her. She turned to find Gage standing at the open passenger door. She looked past him to a stone walkway that led to a covered porch made up of giant logs.

"Where are we?"

He took her arm and pulled her from her seat. "My place."

"What? I told you to take me—"

"I know what you told me." Gage closed the truck door, grabbed her by the elbow and led her up the walk. "But it's four in the morning, the roads are freezing over and my place is closer to the vet…just in case."

Racy pulled from his touch. "I am not staying here."

"You're dead on your feet and I'm not far behind." He turned his back to her and unlocked the massive front door. "Your choice is a warm bed or a cold truck."

"Gage, wait. What will people—"

He disappeared into the house, leaving the door ajar. Racy wrapped her coat around her, already frozen to the core. Warm air flowed from inside. She took a step, then stopped.

She and Gage? Together? They'd worked so hard for months to stay away from each other, and now, to be here at his place…

And what a place it was.

She stepped off the porch. The logs were massive. An angled, high-pitched roof melted into the night sky and rows of dark windows lined one wall. A curved driveway disappeared down the hill to what must be a lower level.

It was bigger than she'd thought he'd build. She'd dreamed about owning this spot of land herself one day, having come here often as a kid. The lake wasn't visible, but judging from his front door it should be—

"Racina Josephine, get your ass in here," Gage bellowed from inside. "You're letting out all the heat."

She jumped and hurried inside. Her heart pounded in her

chest as she closed the door and found herself in a dimly lit entryway. "Gage?"

"In here."

She followed his voice and moved into a vast, open space. Ceilings that reached twenty feet rose above her head. On her left was a gleaming galley-style kitchen partitioned by a bar area. She moved into a combined great room and dining room with floor-to-ceiling windows. A double row of the same windows filled the far wall and she knew the lake was right outside the twin set of French doors. A fire, slowly coming to life in a stone hearth, provided the room's only light.

"Wow."

"Glad you like it." Gage's tone was sharp when he came through a doorway to the left of the fireplace. He'd removed his jacket, but still wore his gun in his shoulder holster, emphasizing the width of his chest. He carried a couple of pillows and a quilt in his arms.

"Did you do this in the few minutes I was outside?"

"I started the fire because I'm cold."

He walked to the long end of the leather L-shaped sectional and dropped the bedding. "I left your backpack, something for you to sleep in and fresh towels in the bathroom. Just leave your clothes on the floor. I'll wash them later."

She looked down. She'd attempted to clean up while at the vet's, but a shower sounded heavenly. "Oh, that's okay. I don't want you to go to any trouble."

He stared at her for a long moment before he turned toward the fireplace. "Fine, I'm too tired to argue with you. The bathroom is through the master bedroom. I'll bunk out here."

Sleep in Gage's bed? Not just no, but hell no.

A shiver raced through her. It wasn't cold in here, despite the size of the room and lack of furnishings. Other than the leather sectional sofa flanked by a couple of free-standing lamps, she could see a flat-screen television and stereo system in one corner. That was it. The dining area was empty except for a large iron chandelier.

She folded her arms across her chest. "Don't you have a spare bedroom I could use?"

"No." He tossed another log on the fire.

He must have at least one other bedroom. This place was huge. "How many bedrooms do you have?"

"Three."

Whoa. "And bathrooms?"

"Three." Gage jabbed at the log, sending up a shower of sparks. "And a half. But, except for the master bath, they all still need some work."

Oh, my, this wasn't a bachelor pad. This was a home.

The realization hit her full force, knocking the breath from her lungs. Gage had built a place where he and his wife—*a real wife*—would raise children, celebrate holidays, have family and friends over for birthday parties and cookouts and—

"Look, the only furniture in the house, besides out here, is in my bedroom, so you're going—what's wrong?"

His voice cut through her thoughts. Determined to shut down the whirlwind in her mind and not think about anything but Jack, she avoided his gaze and headed for the door next to the fireplace.

"Nothing. Bathroom's this way?"

"Straight through the bedroom. You've got fifteen minutes."

The quiet emphasis of his words stopped her. "Or what?"

"My shower is big. Big enough for two."

Chapter Five

Racy disappeared into his bedroom with all the dignity she could muster, considering the condition of her hair and clothes. Moments later, Gage heard the faint sound of running water. He instantly thought back to that morning in Vegas when he'd stood outside another door and imagined her standing beneath a hot spray of water.

Only this time, they were in his house. And she was in his shower.

He backed away from the bedroom door and headed for the stairs to the lower level of the house. He did a quick check of the rooms, came back upstairs and reset the security system at the front door. He then stored his weapon in a concealed but accessible location in the living room.

When he heard the water shut off he looked at his watch. Twenty-five minutes. Refusing to consider if she'd stayed in the shower longer on purpose, he waited another ten minutes, making sure nothing but silence came from behind the closed door.

His own shower was quick, his eyes straying to the curves beneath the blankets on his bed as he grabbed her soiled clothes on the way out. In the laundry room, he shoved her clothes into the washing machine. Then something pink, a scrap of lace and string at his feet, caught his eye.

Racy's underwear.

It only took a second before he realized the panties were the same pair he'd seen hanging from that hideous trophy the morning they'd woken up married in Vegas. The memories returned and his lower half snapped to attention like a raw recruit. He tossed the panties into the machine, went into his living room and sank into the soft leather cushions of his couch.

Damn, it had been one hell of a day.

He propped his bare feet on the table, stared into the orange and yellow flames of the fire and let his mind wander back to the night's events.

After Racy's show on the bar he'd gone downstairs, keeping to the outer edges of the crowd. From the shadows of a booth he'd kept an eye on both Racy and his sister while quieting the rumble in his belly with a supersize burger and fries.

Landon Cartwright had walked by and stopped to introduce his brother, in town for Landon and Maggie's upcoming wedding. Gage had been suspicious of Cartwright when he'd come to town six months ago, but he'd proved to be a good man and Gage now considered him a friend. He recognized Landon's brother as the cowboy Racy had picked to enjoy her special drink. He'd returned Chase Cartwright's firm handshake, refusing to acknowledge the relief he felt that this guy would soon head back to Texas.

And while he still didn't understand Gina's desire to

work at The Blue Creek, he'd sure as hell pissed her off by showing up tonight. That's okay, he was pissed, too. At himself because foremost in his mind was another woman and the fact that he was still married to her, when he should be focused on his family.

"Isn't that a kick in the head?" He said to the dancing flames. "Married to a woman who can't stand the sight of you?"

Gage's eyes burned with fatigue, but sleep wouldn't come. The jumbled thoughts in his head wouldn't allow it.

Hell, who was he kidding? His houseguest wouldn't allow it.

The moment Racy had fallen asleep after they'd left the veterinary clinic, he'd headed to his house. There was no way he would take her back to deal with her loser brothers. Of course, he hadn't thought much past that decision until they'd gotten to his front door. He'd found himself aiming twice to get the key in the lock as images of Racy's flame-red hair and naked skin against the dark sheets of his king-size bed filled his head.

Damn, it was hot in here.

He didn't know if it was the fire or the flannel pajama pants, an old habit from living with his family he'd broken once he'd moved out. Going from the shower to his bed naked had quickly become the norm.

Not tonight. Tonight, there was a sexy-as-all-get-out woman curled up in his bed. And not just any woman. His wife.

He'd thought he'd seen a flash of something—passion, maybe—in her eyes when he'd called her Mrs. Steele back in her office. But when she'd found her matching letter from the Nevada bar association, she'd looked more like she was going to be sick to her stomach.

Other than a strained silence or biting retorts, they

hadn't discussed what they were going to do about the fact they were still legally married.

Gage grabbed the mail he'd dumped on the coffee table when he'd first walked in. He opened a heavy white envelope. A handwritten note fell from the card inside. He angled it toward the fire to read the delicate writing.

Dear Gage,
Since you're a member of the wedding party, you already have this information, but it's only fair you get an invite in case you want to bring a date.

Yeah, right. Thanks to his work schedule and being a hands-on contractor for this place, the last time he'd been on a date was well over a year ago. Not counting Vegas, of course.

Your friendship has always meant so much to me and now to Landon, as well. Thanks for being part of our special day.
Love, Maggie and Landon
P.S. I promise I won't pair up you and Racy!

He crushed the note and tossed it into the fire. Rising, he walked around the end of the couch and stopped when he reached the glass doors that led to the two-level deck he'd put the final nail in last month. The storm clouds had blown away. A full moon shined down on the snow and re-flected in the dark, glasslike surface of the lake.

He thought again about the last line of the note. *You and Racy.* Except for that lost weekend five months ago, there'd never been a "him and Racy."

No, that wasn't true.

Years ago, on a spring night, right here at Echo Lake.

A senior anxious for graduation, he'd come to the lake looking for some quiet time. What he'd found instead was sixteen-year-old Racy Dillon.

He closed his eyes against the memory, but it came anyway.

"Hey there."

She whipped her head around, a mess of red curls flying over her shoulder. *Damn, she was pretty.* Perched on a rock near the edge of the lake, her legs bare except for her once-white sneakers. Cutoff jean shorts revealed miles of skin, and a white collared shirt outlined her breasts. Racy Dillon had filled out with curves in all the right places early on.

So had her reputation, but he didn't believe half the stuff the guys boasted about her in the locker room. The other half? Well, she never seemed to be lonely.

"What the hell are you doing here?" She pressed whatever she was holding close to her chest.

He leaned against the closest tree. "Looking for some peace and quiet. Like you."

"Without your posse of hanger-ons?" She glanced around as if looking for a crowd. "Gee, I didn't know you could stand your own company."

Gage shook his head. Being the sheriff's eldest son and the captain of the football team, most of the kids spent more time sucking up to him than anything else. Not Racy. Last year, she'd called him out on a wrong answer in front of everyone in English lit, despite her being a freshman in an upper-level class, and she hadn't backed down since.

Neither did he. "Yeah, and you're here with your friends."

The pain in her eyes told him he'd hit his mark. "Get lost, Steele."

She turned away and went back to scribbling. He saw it was a notebook she was focusing on. "What are you writing?"

Her head stayed bent over the book. "None of your business."

He grinned. "Fair enough."

A long moment of silence passed before she said, "Aren't you leaving?"

"Not until you tell me."

Her pencil stilled. She raised her head and stared out at the setting sun and the darkening shadows on the blue water. A breeze lifted her hair and floated it across her face. Unlike most girls he knew, she didn't care about her looks.

Maybe because her family never had any money. Not that Destiny was loaded with richies, but it had its pecking order and the Dillon family was at the bottom. Her clothes were secondhand, not that any of the guys cared. Not with those big brown eyes and that flame-red hair that reached her backside.

She finally tucked a long, curly strand behind one ear. "I'm writing about the lake."

He blinked. "You mean a poem or something?"

She turned to him. "Maybe. Right now it's just my thoughts, feelings, words that pop into my head…" She shrugged and offered him a small smile before turning back to her notebook.

His lower half reacted instinctively to the curve of her lips. *Whoa, that never happened before.* Racy, with two older brothers and a father who kept his dad's department on its toes, Racy was just a pain-in-the-ass kid two years behind him in school. Someone fun to tease and trade barbs with, so why was he now—

He stopped the thought before it could form and shoved his hands into his pockets. Silent minutes passed. She was successfully ignoring him. With the sun almost gone from the sky, he knew he should head home, but he wanted to stay. The water and the woods always had a calming effect on him.

He leaned his head back against the rough surface of the tree and stared out over the water. The sky, the lake and the trees all blended together. He had no idea how long he stood there, not really seeing anything, just listening to the sounds of the woods, the increasing winds and Racy's pencil scratching over the paper.

A rumbling caused him to focus on the cloud-filled sky. "Did you hear that?"

Racy didn't reply. Gage was surprised at how dark it had gotten. Another roar came from the dark clouds. "Come on, we'd better get out of here."

"Go, I'm fine," Racy muttered.

"A storm is coming in fast." The first splat of fat rain-drops hit him in the face. "Let's go."

She continued writing. "I can get home by myself."

"How did you get out here?"

"I walked."

"What? It's ten miles from town."

"It's no big deal." She looked up as a boom of thunder crashed over their heads. She jumped, slammed her note-book closed, and hurried off the rock. "Okay, maybe I'll head back."

"My truck's on the other side of the clearing." He grabbed her hand. They needed to get out from under these trees. They kept the rain, falling steady now, off them, but if there was thunder, lightning was sure to follow.

"I'm not going anywhere with you." She tugged free.

Gage grabbed her arm. "Come on, let's go!"

She dug in her heels as they reached the clearing. The wind and the rain lashed at them without the protection of the forest. "What's the matter? This is great! I feel so alive!"

"Getting zapped in the ass by lightning isn't my idea of fun. And this isn't a warm spring rain. It's freezing." He wrapped his arm around her. "Come on!"

The skies opened up and they ran the rest of the way to the truck. By the time they'd crawled into the cab of his restored 1940s pickup they were soaking wet. Panting from the run, their warm breath caused the windows to instantly fog over. He'd grabbed his gray sweat jacket and put it around her shoulders.

"Th-thanks." She pushed away the dark, wet strands clinging to her face and neck. The journal resting on her bare knees. "Oh, my writing. It'll be ruined."

"Put it back here." He grabbed the notebook and slid it behind the seat. It landed, causing a few wobbly pings to echo inside the truck cab. Gage cringed and hoped Racy hadn't heard.

"What was that?"

No such luck. "Ah, nothing." He jammed his key into the ignition and started the engine. "It takes a minute for the heater to warm up."

"What are you hiding, Steele?"

He read suspicion in those beautiful eyes. "I told you. Nothing."

Her eyes narrowed.

"It's…it's my guitar."

Shock replaced suspicion. "You play the guitar?"

His face heated under her gaze. He grabbed at his wet T-shirt and yanked it over his head, blocking her view. "Is that so hard to believe?"

"N-no, I guess not."

He looked at her again. Despite her body turned toward him, their knees practically touching, she seemed intent on staring out the windshield.

Except her eyes kept darting back to look at him, too.

His T-shirt fell to the floor in a sopping puddle. "Sorry, but I was freezing."

"Oh, no, that's okay." Racy's tongue did a quick swipe

over her lips. She started to remove his sweat jacket. "You can have this back if you're cold—"

"No, you keep it." He pulled the soft material back over her shoulders, his fingers catching on her wet skin where the buttons on her shirt had worked free.

Jeez, talk about being zapped.

He let go, but didn't move back behind the steering wheel. He leaned forward and reached past her shoulder, bringing their bodies even closer together. "I'll just get my letterman jacket. It's hanging on your side of the truck."

His fingers closed on the wool and leather material of the jacket as his gaze landed on the swell of her breasts. It took a hard blink for him to look away. She'd turned toward him, her mouth inches from his. He stared at her full pink lips for a long moment before forcing himself to look into her eyes.

"God, I want to kiss you." The words fell from his mouth.

She took another swipe at her lips, turning them shiny wet. It felt like a hundred-pound weight landed on his chest.

"Why?" she breathed.

"Because you're so pretty."

He read disbelief in her eyes. Damn, she must have heard that before. He tightened his grip, one hand on the jacket and one on the dashboard, to keep from pulling her into his arms. He moved in another inch.

"Can I?"

He counted to three. Three times her warm breath touched his skin. Then she nodded and he covered her mouth with his. The trembling of her lips caused him to go slow, slower than he'd ever remembered kissing a girl.

At eighteen, Gage'd had his share of girls, losing his virginity two years earlier. He'd ended things with his girlfriend a few nights ago, not wanting any entanglement before they headed off to separate colleges in the fall.

None of which explained what he was doing sharing a

closed-mouth kiss with Racy Dillon, who was apparently more innocent than everyone thought.

He started to pull back until the warmth of her finger-tips landed on his shoulder. She pressed closer, her hand making its way into the hair at the back of his neck. Her mouth opened and her tongue touched his lips.

All rational thought disappeared.

He pulled her up against him, the cold wetness of her shirt a shock against his heated skin. His mouth opened and his tongue met hers. When her fingers tightened in his hair, he moved back behind the steering wheel, bringing Racy with him. He fitted her onto his lap with his jacket draped over the both of them.

"Oh, Gage, please kiss me again."

For someone who was so innocent a moment ago, she sure picked up on the act of kissing fast. With one arm caught between her shoulder and the steering wheel, his free hand dropped to the curve of her hip and her bare legs. A deep groan filled his chest when she pressed against him. If she kept moving like that, he was going to embarrass both of them real soon. But he couldn't stop kissing her, touching her.

He brought his hand up to the buttons on her shirt. They came undone beneath his nimble fingers. He pushed one wet corner of material off her shoulder, taking her bra strap with it, trailing his lips down her neck and along her skin. Raising his head, he looked at her and found her brown eyes watching him, her lips swollen from his kisses. His fingers slowly moved over the soft fullness of her breast, down to where the plain white material still covered her—

Gage jerked himself from the memory before he got to what had happened next—the sharp raps against the driver's-side window. The leering grin of one of his father's deputies. Racy cowering behind him as he talked. Her icy demand to be taken home.

Damn, he hadn't thought of that afternoon since—okay, since a few weeks ago when he'd stood on his newly stained deck looking out on the same lake.

But it was ancient history, along with the time they'd spent together in Vegas. No matter how many memories returned, rough snatches from years ago or clearly defined moments from five months gone, it was in the past.

Except, of course, he was still married to the woman.

He leaned against the door frame, thumbs tucked into the waistband of his pants. Cold seeped into his skin, but a burning desire for the one woman he couldn't have raged inside him.

Time, distance and maturity had made it easier to turn his craving into a sometimes friendly, sometimes antagonistic game of one-upmanship she seemed to enjoy as much as he did.

Hell, the crazy idea to ask her out on a real date had popped into his head more than once over the years, especially after the fog of his father's death had lifted. Just to see if there was something between them.

Except life always seemed to get in the way. Whether it was busting her brothers for drug trafficking or her second marriage and subsequent divorce a year and a half later, life hadn't given them a break.

And those events had seemed to sap the fire from her.

Oh, she'd flirted and teased, but it wasn't the same. It was only last summer that she finally seemed more like herself. Then she'd melted into his arms in a dim corner of the hotel bar in Vegas, responding with a passion he'd never experienced with any other woman. And he'd been a goner. Again.

"Gage?"

Her warm, sexy voice eased past his broken defenses. His fingers curled into fists, pulling the soft material of his pants even tighter across his erection. No turning around now. "What do you want, Racy?"

Silence filled the air. Gage's fertile brain came up with a variety of answers and all of them ended with the two of them horizontal.

"Nothing," she finally said.

"Then go back to sleep."

She moved farther into the room and her reflection caught in the glass. Wrapped from her shoulders to her feet in one of his mother's handmade quilts, she sat on the short end of the sectional that faced the fireplace. "I'm not tired. Ya know, I never thanked you for what you did tonight...for Jack."

He looked over his shoulder and watched her snuggle into the cushions of the sofa and prop her legs on the coffee table. The deep blue material of the quilt gave way, revealing bare skin from her toes to midthigh. He concentrated on her profile, trying to ignore the fact she wasn't wearing the bottom half of the pajamas he'd left for her.

Was she wearing the top?

"And for what you didn't do to my brothers," she added with a sigh.

He turned back to the night sky and released a deep breath, fogging the window. "Why are you lying for them?"

He watched in the window's reflection as she dropped her head back against the couch. "Force of habit? And since this conversation is strictly off the record, they did break in, but I'm not pressing charges and I don't have to give a reason why."

Nothing like talking about ex-cons to put a damper on his arousal. Gage crossed his arms over his chest, but still didn't turn around. "Their paperwork says they've been out for three weeks."

She swung around. "I had no idea. I swear it."

"So why are they back in Destiny?"

"This is their home."

"Yeah, they did quite a number on *your* home."

Racy stared at the fire. "So I noticed."

He heard the despair in the clipped response and couldn't stop from looking at her again. "What're you going to do?"

"Clean it up. Like always."

"And let them stay?"

She tightened the blanket around her and crossed her legs at the ankles. "Like Billy Joe said, where else would they go? I know what you think of my brothers. Yes, what they did to Jack was stupid, but I don't think they purposely meant to hurt him."

"How can you defend them?"

"Because they're my family." Her voice caught and she paused. "The only family I've got left. Look at you. You spent today cleaning up after the twins and trying to get Gina fired."

"What Garrett and Giselle did was stupid and dangerous, but you can't possibly compare drag racing to being part of a statewide drug trafficking ring."

"Of course not. But my brothers have served their time and while I had hoped prison had pounded some sense into those thick skulls of theirs, I didn't for one minute mistake them for upstanding and perfect citizens. Like you."

He turned fully to face her now, having regained control over his body. "I'm not perfect. Just honest."

"And this is me being honest. I don't know what I'm going to do about Billy Joe and Justin. I do know I don't have to decide at o-dark-thirty in the morning." She paused for a long moment. "Can we change the subject, please?"

She was right. Now wasn't the time to talk about her brothers. Hell, at the moment they were legally *his* brothers-in-law. Yee-haw on that.

He should send her back to bed, but instead he asked, "Been in college long?"

She turned, pushing long waves of red hair, still damp from the shower, from her face.

Damn high school memories.

"How did you—ah, my books. Yeah, I've been taking classes for years. More off than on, but when my last husband walked out with the little amount left in my bank—"

"I am your last husband, Mrs. Steele." *Okay, he should've let that go, too. What was with him tonight?*

"Why do you keep calling me that?"

She studied him and his skin burned every place her gaze touched. So much for control. He found himself thankful his position left him somewhat in the shadows. "Because it gets a rise out of you?"

"Well, knock it off." The tip of her tongue snaked out to swipe across her lips. "Anyway, when Tommy took off, I decided it was time to plan for my future. I graduate in a few weeks."

Gage forced himself to concentrate on the flare of pride in his gut at her achievement, not the wet shine of her mouth. "Good for you. What's your major?"

"Business administration."

"Plan to move on to bigger and better things than The Blue Creek?"

The fire in the fireplace was no match for the blaze in her eyes. "What does that mean?"

Whoa, what'd he say? "I figured you wouldn't stick around—"

"And why's that?" She jerked upright and her feet dropped to the floor. "Is working in a bar only for stupid people?"

Chapter Six

"That's not what I meant."

Racy knew that, but Gage's questions about her brothers rubbed her the wrong way. So did lying between his sheets, the towel she'd used after her shower and the too big pajamas he'd left on the sink.

Why? Because they all smelled exactly the same.

Exactly like Gage.

One deep whiff and her head filled with memories of shared showers and shared sheets back in Vegas. And the shared vows that made them man and wife.

Damn, they really needed to talk about this still-married mess, but first things first.

"What's wrong, Gage? Can't understand why a college-educated woman would want to work in a bar? Oh, wait—how would that explain your sister being my newest employee?"

"We're not talking about my sister." He moved forward

to grip the back of the leather sectional sofa that separated them. "But I can't deny I don't want her working there."

"I don't really think you have a say in the matter."

He tensed, then sighed. "I just don't get it."

"What's there to get? She wants to meet people and wear sexy makeup."

Gage snorted. "Yeah, I saw your handiwork tonight."

"The view from the balcony is amazing, isn't it?"

He froze for a moment, then straightened and turned, resting his hip against the cushioned back of the couch. "It has its advantages, but you knew that when you pulled that stunt."

"Glad you enjoyed the show." She stood and walked to the fireplace. "Or did you?"

"You were damn lucky with the cowboy you picked. Unlike last time."

A shiver of fear had run through Racy when she'd first stretched out on the bar. The last guy she'd performed a Racy Special with had looked clean-cut and nicely dressed, too, but had a predatory gleam in his eye she hadn't seen until it was too late. When he'd crawled up on the bar informing her in a lecherous snarl he was a former cellmate of her brother's, her blood had run cold.

Thank goodness her bouncers had got there before things had turned really ugly. But tonight she'd pressed on, secure in the knowledge it was Landon's brother with her. Maggie's intended groom was a stand-up kind of guy. Chase was, too. He hadn't laid a hand on her.

"So what was that? Some kind of payback?"

Gage's question yanked Racy from her musings. "What?"

"I'll admit the dancing was a nice surprise. I'm sure the male patrons—hell, I'll bet even some females in the audience enjoyed it. But the 'Special'? You spent more time staring up into the rafters than paying attention to that cowboy—"

She whirled. Her body blocked the light from the hearth, leaving Gage in the shadows. "You think I did that for you?"

"Gina told you I'd been spending time on the balcony and you just couldn't resist. I think you have more in common with Tammy than you think."

"In common with—" The comparison to her waitress who was more breasts than brains brought a swift and unexpected jab of pain to her chest. She didn't know why she cared what this man thought of her, but she did. "I am not a tease."

"Of course you are. Always have been, always will be." Gage shrugged with careless effort. "Doesn't matter if it's dancing on top of the bar, at the diner…in my living room."

"Your living—I am not teasing you!" She skirted the end of the sofa and headed straight for him, clutching the blanket around her like a cape. "And I don't tease. I flirt. There's a difference."

The fire lit one side of his face, emphasizing the darkness of his eyes and the firm set of his mouth. The other half remained in the shadows as his gaze made the journey over the worn material that covered her to her toes.

Thankfully he couldn't see how revealing the V-neck of his pajama top was or how the hem ended high on her thighs, narrowly covering her bare bottom, but her skin burned anyway.

She stared back at miles of gorgeous skin, defined muscles and just a smattering of dark hair that faded above his belly button before it appeared again, a straight line into the low waistband of his flannel pants. Talk about a tease.

"There a difference?" His tone held phony innocence. "Please explain."

"A flirt is having fun, being playful, offering a hint of what could be, depending on who's on the receiving end. It's harmless."

"Harmless?"

She kept talking over his question. "A tease is someone who gets a person all worked up, but doesn't follow through. Someone who makes a promise, then reneges. Who makes the other person believe they're going to—you know—but then they stop."

"Like I said, you're a tease."

"Gage, how can you say that? I haven't even touched you tonight!"

He grabbed her and a heartbeat later she was nestled between his legs. Her hands landed against his chest, the heat of his skin searing her fingertips. The blanket fell from her shoulders to gather at her hips, where his hands held her tight against the hard, hot ridge of him.

"Do you think you have to touch me?" The rasp of his voice dragged over her skin like the coarse wool of a thick sweater. "Don't you know it's just the sight of you? The bounce of your curls? The sway in your hips or the sparkle in your eyes?"

Words of protest died on her lips when he pulled her even closer. One hand sank into her hair, holding her in place as he leaned in, his mouth at her hairline.

He dragged in a deep, gutted breath, his voice a rough whisper. "It's this warm vanilla-lime scent that surrounds you, even now, fresh from the shower. Hell, Racina...you don't even have to be in the room to tease me. Just the memory of holding you in my arms, covering your body with mine."

Racy reeled. His lips moved over her forehead, his words having a hypnotic effect on her. This was madness. That was as clear to her as the fact they were alone in his house with nothing separating them except a couple of layers of material.

And a history of being on opposite sides of everything. Her fingers bit into his chest, her nails digging at his skin. A soft moan escaped her lips. The desire to taste, to press her mouth to his heated flesh threatened to consume her. He leaned back and placed a finger beneath her chin. With gentle pressure, he forced her to look at him.

"I remember every second of that night in Vegas. From the moment you won that damn trophy to when I woke up to find you, standing naked, clutching our wedding announcement. The memories are crystal clear. Tell me I'm not the only one...tell me—"

"I remember."

Her affirmation came out in a strangled sob he took into his mouth when he kissed her. He cupped the back of her head and thrust his tongue past her lips, to be met full force with hers. A roaring filled her ears at his eagerness. At hers.

The memories of them together last summer swirled inside her head, springing back to life in a bright burst of rainbow Technicolor, now that she was in his arms again.

He angled her head, deepening the kiss. The dusky flavor of his mouth danced over her tongue as they tasted each other. Her hands brushed against his chest and collarbone until they circled his neck. He removed his hands from her waist to let the quilt fall to the floor. Then they returned, fisting the cotton fabric of the pajama top. He lifted it, baring her backside to the night air.

He pulled her up tight against him and she rose on her tiptoes and rotated her hips, so tempted to push him backward and topple the two of them down into the soft leather cushions below. From there it would only take a few tugs on his pajama pants to release him and ease onto the hardness she'd committed to memory even after all these months—

A loud buzzing had him jerking back, releasing her from his hold. She stepped away, reality rushing in.

This was wrong.

She shouldn't be doing this. They shouldn't be doing

this. Sex wasn't going to solve anything. Hell, with everything else between them it would only make things worse.

"What—what was that?" she asked.

"Ah, that was a sanity check."

"What?"

He closed his eyes for a moment, then pulled in a deep breath. "It's my washing machine."

"You're washing my clothes?"

"Yeah." He opened his eyes. "You'll need clean clothes when it comes time to get dressed."

She didn't speak, but her breasts rose and fell as she tried to control her erratic breathing. Did she read an invitation in his eyes? An overpowering longing to get naked and leave the worrying about clean clothes for later?

Was that longing mirrored in her eyes?

He closed the distance between them and dipped his head, but stopped. His gaze moved from her eyes to her lips and back again. "I'm gonna take care of the laundry." His words were a soft whisper. "You should get into bed and— ah, try to get some sleep."

"Now who's being a tease?"

"I am, Mrs. Steele. It sucks, doesn't it?"

She opened her mouth to protest, but he pressed a finger against her lips. "Don't. You're really good at this game, Racy. So am I. But I'm tired of playing with you."

The first thing she saw when she opened her eyes was a scrap of pink lace, neatly folded, atop a tidy stack of clean clothes perched on the bed next to her.

Oh, damn.

A low moan vibrated deep in her throat as she covered her face with her hand, blocking both the sunshine that poured in from the bay window and the sight of her panties. She rolled into a mountain of pillows and breathed deeply, pulling in a clean, outdoorsy scent that spoke of fresh air, deep woods and crystal clear lake water. Gage's scent.

She peeked between her fingers at her clothes. He'd done it. He'd actually washed, dried and folded her entire outfit, right down to that silly scrap of lace and strings. He'd told her as much last night, but her mind had been so jumbled with everything they'd talked about.

And there was that kiss. That amazing, soul-shaking, knee-knocking, world-tilting kiss.

She hadn't resisted when he'd pulled her into his arms, his whispered words hot on her skin. With every touch and every syllable, he'd pulled her in deeper and deeper and she'd gone willingly. His revelation that he remembered every moment of their time together in Vegas had lulled her into admitting the same.

Damn, damn and double damn!

She'd been so careful in not divulging that she remembered anything. Besides being scared Gage would use it against her, she'd been embarrassed at her behavior, too much alcohol or not. Then again, she hadn't been the only one doing the kissing and touching and oh, so much more, that night.

But it had been more than just the sex.

Before they'd even got to the suite, they'd shared a magical night. They'd talked about everything from movies to politics to music. The only thing they hadn't talked about was home. An unspoken agreement between them not to talk about the past or the future. Living in the moment had been enough.

They'd danced and shopped and laughed until they'd cried at a hilarious ventriloquist-comedian. They'd walked the Strip from hotel to hotel, including the one with the enormous fountain she couldn't resist dipping her toes into.

Hours later, they'd ended up outside a jewelry store.

Gage had been looking at the window displays, but it was the bride and groom emerging from the nearby chapel that captured her attention. The look of pure love and happiness on their faces slammed straight into her heart. She'd never experienced that with either of her two husbands and she wanted to feel that joy for the first time in her life.

And she wanted it with the man standing next to her.

She'd slipped inside the store and returned minutes later with matching rings. Gage's teasing had disappeared when she'd opened the velvet box—

Racy pushed the memories from her mind.

No, she wasn't taking this trip down memory lane. None of that mattered, not anymore. Gage had made it clear last night that, while she turned him on, he wasn't interested.

And they hadn't even discussed what they would do about their so-called marriage. Was another annulment— a real one this time—doable? Did that include a trip back to Vegas? Was it possible to keep an uncontested divorce out of Destiny's gossip mill?

Death, desertion and now divorce.

The deadly three. Wyatt had died on her, Tommy had walked out for greener pastures and now Gage.

Jeez, could she be any more of a loser? No wonder the man wasn't interested in playing—much less anything else—with her.

She glanced at her watch and groaned again. Almost eleven. She never slept this late. There was no way she would meet up with Maggie and Leeann in an hour. She needed to pick up Jack, see what condition her house was in and deal with her brothers.

Rolling over, she grabbed her backpack from the floor. Maggie would still be at church. She punched Leeann's number into her cell phone and waited.

"Leeann Harris speaking."

"Hey, it's me." Racy pushed her hair off her face, not even wanting to think about what style her riot of wild curls formed. "Did I wake you?"

"Are you kidding? I logged in 10K before 9:00 a.m."

Racy groaned. Her friend was a running machine. She didn't know how she did it. "You make me sick. At least tell me you did it while watching the boob tube."

"On a day like this?" Leeann's voice raised an octave. "With all that snow and sunshine? It's gorgeous even if it's barely above freezing. Don't tell me your ass is still in bed."

She kicked at the dark blue sheets that matched Gage's eyes and stood. "No, I'm up."

"Hmm, I'll bet. Did Maggie tell you about lunch today?"

She leaned across the bed and grabbed her clothes. "That's why I'm calling. I have to—"

"Hold on, someone's beeping. Let me make sure it's not my boss. I'm not on the schedule today, but when you work for the sheriff—be right back."

Silence filled the air. Racy doubted it was Gage calling Leeann. She strained, but didn't hear a sound coming from the living room. A glance at the thick log walls of his bedroom revealed the reason why.

She quickly pulled on her panties. Okay, jeans next. Damn, they were still warm. She blamed the sunshine. It was easier than thinking Gage had just removed them from the dryer. Easier than trying to pull the denim material over her hips while balancing the cell phone between her ear and shoulder. Ah, success.

"Hi, I'm back. Maggie's here, too."

"It's about time you woke up," Maggie's voice sailed over the three-way call. "Were you stuck at the bar due to the weather? You never picked up this morning."

Racy's stomach dropped to her feet, her fingers frozen on the undone zipper of her jeans. "You called the house?"

Were her brothers still at her place? If so, was it brains or booze that kept them from answering the telephone?

"To see if you wanted a lift to church. Don't think I haven't noticed you slipping in the back the last few weeks."

Spiritual renewal was the furthest thing from Racy's mind at the moment. Right now, she needed to keep her friends away from her place until she knew what was going on.

"I was going to suggest we move up our lunch and leave right from church," Maggie continued, "and pick up Miss I-Communicate-With-God-In-My-Own-Way together."

Leeann huffed at the nickname. "Hey, I get more from my runs in the great outdoors than from a preacher lecturing about the sins of man."

"Ah, guys, our lunch plans are why I'm calling." Racy grabbed her fringed top and shoved it in her backpack. Her sweatshirt would work fine, but first things first.

She headed for the window, determined to find a way to release the simple Roman shades. The reflection off the mounds of fresh snow jacked up what promised to be a whopper of a headache. "I'm sorry, but I have to bail."

"What?"

"Why?"

Her friends' voices overlapped. Racy prayed she could get out of this with the smallest lie possible. She reached for the shade's tension string when movement caught her eye.

Gage stood in the center of a plant-filled, glass-enclosed sunroom. Bright sunshine bounced off shiny green leaves and sweat-sheened muscles. Facing away from her, he bowed deep at the waist, his pajama pants tight across his backside.

Then he rose and started a series of fluid arm and leg movements, each pose moving gracefully from one into the next, as muscles flexed and stretched. She recognized it as a martial art called Tai Chi. And Gage did it with perfection.

"Hello?"

"Racy?"

"Ah, yeah…I'm still here." She tried to swallow, but her mouth was dry. Her eyes locked on the controlled power of Gage's body, thankful he continued to face away from her.

"What's going on?" Leeann demanded. "You sound weird."

"Landon's pulling up to the house," Maggie said. "I'll kick the family out of the car—that's said with love, dear—and Lee, I'll pick you up in fifteen minutes. Racy, we're coming over."

"No, you can't." Panic filled her. "I don't want you guys at the house."

"Did you do something stupid last night?" Maggie demanded. "Chase was a perfect gentleman, but if you took your plan a step in the wrong direction—"

"Hey, what plan?"

"There was no plan," Racy said to Leeann, and before Maggie could counter her she pushed on. "I just had a rough night and things are crazy."

"How rough?" Leeann cut in again. "Are you in trouble? Do you need help, official or otherwise? I can be there before Maggie even hits the highway. With backup, and it won't be Steele because he's off duty."

"Maybe she wants you to call Gage." Maggie said.

"Are you nuts? She can't stand the man."

"There's a thin line between love and hate. If you ask me it's long past time she marched across that line."

"Not everyone is looking for happily ever after, Mags."

"Just because you're not doesn't mean Racy feels the same."

Racy pinched the bridge of her nose and closed her eyes. "Can I get a word in?"

"As long as it's the truth," Maggie shot back.

What the hell? Her friends weren't going to rest until they found out everything.

"Gage gave me a ride home because the weather sucked, okay? I found my brothers at the house celebrating their early release from prison by getting themselves and my dog drunk, which resulted in Gage again playing chauffeur for a trip to Kali's clinic. We finally got to bed about an hour before dawn."

The words fell from her mouth before she could stop them. Thank goodness for the need to breathe or otherwise she might've spewed out everything. Including Vegas.

Silence reigned. Racy started a ten count, knowing what was coming.

"Alone?"

She'd only made it to six. "Yes, Mags, alone."

"Are you still there?" Leeann asked. "And I'm guessing this is his new place at the lake?"

"Yes and yes. Before you ask, I didn't know about my brothers' release, and Jack is going to be okay."

Her gaze returned to the action outside in time to see Gage turn to face the beautiful blue waters of the lake. His back fully to her, he continued his workout. It was only a matter of time before his next move had him facing the window where she stood. She couldn't continue to watch—well, yeah she could—but it wouldn't look good.

She started to back away when she spotted her beloved golden retriever, tongue lolling out of his mouth and warm brown eyes fixed on the man who'd rescued him.

"Jack!" she cried. "He's here!"

Her friends started firing questions at her again, but a sharp whistle from her lips stopped them. "Guys, I appreciate the concern and I know you want to talk, but I've got a lot to deal with," Racy begged. "Can we hook up later in the week?"

"My bachelorette party is Friday night. I want details," Maggie demanded.

"I know." Racy attacked the buttons on the pajama top, yanking them open. She had to get dressed and check for herself Jack was okay. "I'll be there."

"If Billy Joe and Justin give you any trouble—" Leeann cut off her words. "If you need help, with anything, please call."

"Thanks, hon. Later, girls."

She snapped the cell phone closed as the last button on the pajama top gave way. She looked up, wanting to see Jack again, but instead found herself locked in the sights of a very sweaty and sexy sheriff.

Busted.

He stood in the center of the sunroom, his chest rising and falling in a steady rhythm. Moisture plastered his hair to his forehead and covered his chest. A perfect set of washboard abs graced his stomach and his pajama pants had slipped past his hip bones. And here she stood in undone jeans and an open pajama top, *his* pajama top, and her hair almost certainly a wild explosion of curls.

I am not a tease.

Of course you are. Always have been, always will be.

Their words filled her head as Gage grabbed a towel from a nearby chair. He hooked it around his neck, never taking his eyes off her.

A quick tug on the string and the shade dropped. Racy headed for the bed, yanking off the pajama top. She had to get dressed. Now.

A deep woof made her freeze.

Too late.

If Jack was in the bedroom, so was Gage.

Chapter Seven

"Eat."

Racy looked at the plate placed in the center of her desk. Four mini-burgers, still sizzling from the grill, topped with pale-green-and-orange coleslaw peeking from sesame seed buns. Golden-brown fried potato wedges sat piled in between the burgers. Their spicy fragrance caused her stomach to rumble.

Twenty-four hours had passed since her last meal. She'd begged off breakfast at Gage's, grateful she'd managed to get out of his place relatively unscathed.

He hadn't followed her dog into the bedroom. She'd yanked on her sweatshirt before turning around, but found only Jack sitting there. When she'd made her way into the living room, Gage had been nothing but cool and detached as he relayed Kali's instructions. Then he'd disappeared into his bedroom to shower before taking her and Jack to get her car.

In fact, the only emotion he'd shown at all was a raised eyebrow and the tightening of his grip on the steering wheel when she'd refused his offer to follow her home.

"Don't say you aren't hungry," a deep, rugged voice interrupted her thoughts. "Your stomach tells another story."

Racy looked up. Justin took a step back, wiping his hands on a dishrag. It still threw her to think he and Billy Joe were out of jail and back home.

The middle child, Justin was older than her by two years. He would've graduated with Gage if he'd stayed in high school instead of dropping out. Based on the few old pictures she had of their father as a young man, Justin was his spitting image, from the slim build to the dark hair to the surly expression.

"What's this?" she asked.

"Lunch." His eyes strayed to the wall clock. "Or dinner. Hell, call it a snack."

"Where'd it come from?"

She was sitting in her office on a Sunday afternoon playing with her crew's schedule, because Ernie, her top-notch cook, and Tammy, her not-so-smart waitress, had taken off for a spur-of-the-moment elopement. At least they'd gone to Reno. But their impromptu trip over the matrimony falls left her up a creek. Her kitchen staff was suffering. Thank goodness Gina had agreed to come in and help handle the Sunday football play-offs crowd.

"The kitchen."

"What were you doing in the kit—"

"Helping." He shoved the dishrag into a back pocket and crossed his arms over his chest. "Things are so crazy back there no one questioned me when I picked up a spatula. I told you this morning when you got home I've changed."

Racy had to talk to her staff about security. "Last night notwithstanding."

"I explained all that. And I apologized."

Yes, he had. The first time she ever remembered any male member of her family doing so.

She'd pulled into her snow-covered driveway, surprised to see the cars gone and the path to the front porch cleared. It had taken a few deep breaths before she'd opened the front door, but once inside she'd found an immaculate house with not a beer bottle or dirty dish in sight.

Jack had sniffed around the living room while Justin had explained he'd awakened before dawn to find Billy Joe and their guests gone. He had then spent the next five hours cleaning up the night's mess, including scrubbing her kitchen floor and tearing out the aged shagged carpet, claiming it was beyond repair.

She'd been stunned. Her place never looked that good when she cleaned. Heck, it never looked that good, period.

Her stomach rumbled again and she grabbed a potato wedge, popping it into her mouth. "Wow," she mumbled as a tangy flavor burst on her tongue. "Don't tell me Tiny came up with this?"

"Your other so-called cook?" Justin snorted. "That guy is lucky he can find the stove beneath that oversize gut of his. Those are mine."

"Hey, Tiny has worked here for years. Yeah, he's stuck on the basics, but this isn't a four star—did you say 'yours'?" Racy looked at the plate again. She couldn't resist snagging another wedge. "As in, you cooked this?"

"As in, the recipe's mine. So is the special slaw on the burgers. Try one."

Racy heard the obscure pride in her brother's voice. She grabbed one of the mini-burgers, noting the size was perfect for her grip, unlike the supersize burgers the cowboys preferred. "I usually have only pickles on my burgers."

"Try it," Justin drawled. "Otherwise I'll feed it to Jack."

At the sound of his name, the golden retriever thumped his tail against the leather couch. Justin had actually gotten down on one knee and apologized to the animal before offering to pay for any vet bills. Racy wasn't sure she believed him, but Jack had offered a wet kiss of forgiveness.

"Jack is on a restricted diet for a few days," she said.

"I was kidding. Now, try it."

She took a bite and fell in love. "This is amazing. Where'd you learn to do this?"

Justin stared at her, his left eyebrow arched high.

Damn, was that expression something little boys learned in school while girls were off playing hopscotch? Gage had done the same exact thing this morning.

She pushed the lawman from her head, determined to focus on her brother as she realized where he'd learned his culinary skill. "In prison? You've got to be kidding."

"I worked my way up from dishwasher until I was prepping for a good ol' Southern boy from Cajun country. Then I started messing around with my own techniques. Like I told you this morning, I've spent the seven years I was stuck in the pen doing something to change my life."

Racy stared at the burger, unable to believe her brother was really its creator. "And Billy Joe?"

"He continued as before. I kept saying no when he tried to get me involved. It took a couple of years, but he finally listened. We didn't talk after that. I didn't even know he'd been released the same day as me until we met at out-processing. I had no idea where I was heading when I left but he'd lined up a ride—" Justin cut off his words. "You've already heard this."

Racy nodded and took another bite. The sweet taste of the coleslaw mixed with the flavorful meat in a perfect combination. "This really is wonderful."

"So you'll hire me?"

The burger caught in her throat and she choked. She grabbed the water bottle her brother had brought in with the food, and forced the bite down with a rush of cold liquid. "What?"

"I need a job, Racy, and you need a cook."

She didn't know what to say. This wasn't something she'd expected in a million years. First the sheriff's sister and now her ex-con brother? She took another large gulp from the water bottle.

"I'm good at this," his voice dropped low as he leaned over the desk, his hands braced on the scarred wood. "I figured after I got out I'd scrape up a job at a greasy spoon somewhere, but this is perfect—"

"Perfect?" Racy shot back. "How am I going to explain an ex-drug-runner slapping hamburger patties in my kitchen? I've got plans for this place—for my future—and they don't include getting shut down because you've decided to revert to old ways."

"I told you—"

"And I'm just supposed to believe you? We haven't seen each other in years and, bam, you're asking for a job? We have no idea what Billy Joe is up to, but you've always followed him in the past. Why should it be any different now?"

"Because I'm different." Justin leaned closer, the muscles in his upper arms straining against the simple white T-shirt he wore. "I've spent years caged like an animal, fighting and scrapping to make something of myself. Yeah, I blew it spending the last few weeks partying with Billy Joe, then breaking in and trashing your house. This morning I knew I had to take control—"

"Hey, Racy—oops, sorry, I wasn't aware you had company." Gina poked her head into the office, her bright blue eyes moving quickly between her and Justin. "I wanted to let you know I'm here and Tiny is threatening to take a meat cleaver to the deep fryer. That can't possibly be a good thing, right?"

Justin straightened and crossed his arms over his chest again. Racy sighed, dropping the burger to her plate and her head to her hands.

"Well?" he asked.

She looked at her brother. "This is a trial period. If Ernie wises up and leaves Tammy at the altar, he could be back here before closing."

"Got it."

Racy looked at Gina again and got a sinking in the pit of her stomach. Oh, no. That wasn't feminine interest she saw in Gina's gaze roaming over Justin's backside?

Not now, not from this girl.

Gage wouldn't just accuse Racy of playing games this time. No, he'd run her out of town on a rail.

"Ah, Gina, this is my brother, Justin."

Gina's eyes met Racy's and she blushed. "Hello."

Justin nodded in her direction, but his gaze returned quickly to Racy.

"I don't remember Racy having any brothers." Gina's smile slipped at Justin's insolence. "Have you always lived in town?"

"He's just moved back this weekend," Racy said. "He's gonna be helping in the kitchen until—well, until the craziness passes."

The stiffness in Justin's shoulders eased and he dropped his hands. "I'll check on Tiny. Enjoy your food."

He turned on his heels and headed for the door the same moment Gina stepped inside. They bumped into each other and Justin sprang back as if he'd been burned, landing hard against the doorjamb.

"Oh, you okay?" Gina reached out, but Justin skirted

the door frame and slid into the hall, a paperback falling to the floor.

Gina got to it first. "*Songs of a Worker* by Arthur O'Shaughnessy?" She read the title aloud.

Justin took the book and shoved it into his back pocket. "Just some light reading."

Then he was gone.

Racy sighed, knowing she had to nip this attraction in the bud. "Gina, maybe it's none of my business, but please don't—"

The shrill ring of the phone cut off her words. She grabbed the receiver. "Yes? Okay, I'll be right there."

"Is something else wrong?" Gina asked.

"Only if my luck hasn't changed." Racy moved from behind her desk, making a mental note to warn off her newest waitress about Justin later. Of course, once her brother found out Gina's last name, that wouldn't be an issue. "I've got a visitor out front. You okay working two nights in a row?"

"Sure," Gina said, following her. "And I forbade Gage to show up tonight."

Racy faltered. "You saw your brother?"

"He came to the house for Sunday dinner, as usual. I took great pleasure in ignoring him until you called. Thanks for getting me out of there."

Before Racy could respond further, they entered the main bar. Gina went in one direction while a table of customers beckoned for Racy's attention. She stopped to say hello, then moved toward the swinging doors that led to the foyer. The doors opened and a woman, dressed in dark slacks and a cashmere wool trench coat, walked in. She slowly pulled leather gloves from her fingers. Not a hair on her head was out of place.

Donna Pearson. Head of Destiny's Betterment Committee, a royal pain in the ass and the last thing Racy needed right now.

She headed toward her, knowing the low-cut neckline on her Blue Creek T-shirt would drive the older woman nuts. She guessed only ten years separated them in age, but they were light-years apart in every other way.

"Mrs. Pearson, what can I do for you?"

Donna wrinkled her nose. She took her time looking around the bar, her gaze pausing on the waitresses near the dance floor before she focused on Racy. "Miss Dillon. I'm sure you know why I'm here."

"We're running a bit behind in the kitchen this afternoon—" her ex-con brother at the grill notwithstanding "—but I can draw you a beer if you're looking to wet your whistle."

The woman paled another shade, if that was possible. "My whistle is fine, thank you."

Racy doubted that. "So, what brings you by?"

The woman reached into a leather folder she held and pulled out a sheet of paper. She turned the letter toward Racy. "I assume you and Mr. DeGrasso received this?"

One glance and Racy recognized the letter of complaint that had arrived a few weeks ago. The Destiny Betterment Committee felt Max, as owner of The Blue Creek, and she in particular as manager, were exploiting the Belles, the girls who waited tables and entertained by dancing on the bars.

The committee had recommended the practice cease and desist immediately. Max had laughed it off, but it had fired a burn of resentment in Racy she couldn't extinguish.

"You know he did. I believe in a telephone conversation Max—ah, Mr. DeGrasso stated that while he appreciated the recommendation—" his words, not hers "—he, *we*, decided the entertainment here at The Blue Creek would remain unchanged."

"I had hoped I could change his mind."

"My girls dance on a volunteer basis. It's not an employment requirement. Safety precautions are taken, including a security team, to ensure no one, waitress or customer, is harassed in any way, sexually or otherwise."

The woman's posture stiffened. "It's not just a safety issue, Miss Dillon."

Here it comes.

"I understand the creation of the dancers was your idea."

Racy nodded. "When I became manager four years ago."

"Their attire is wholly too revealing and leaves little to the imagination." Donna's gaze flittered over Racy's cleavage. Her eyes narrowed into slits. "The bars are a poor substitute for a stage and the dance moves are the same thing one would find in one of those…gentlemen's clubs."

Gentlemen's club, strip joint. Same thing.

"My dancers are not strippers, Mrs. Pearson. No clothing is removed other than perhaps a cowboy hat, and there are no poles in the building." She fought to keep her voice calm and low, knowing the girls were close by. "The team performs synchronized dance steps, and works very hard to learn the routines. It's fun, provides physical exercise and for the last three years no one has complained."

"When my husband and I moved to Destiny this summer, I took it upon myself to join forces with like-minded citizens who wish to preserve what is good and wholesome and drive out—"

Racy's hands tightened into fists. "As I said, we've had no complaints. Before now."

Donna Pearson's lips thinned into a hard line, then she said, "And that led to your performance last night?"

She should've known her spontaneity would come back to bite her in the ass. Hard. "I join the dancers from time to time."

"You did more than dance last night."

Ah, so she was bothered by that, too. What would Miss High-and-Mighty think if she knew that money was going to the children's area at Destiny's library?

Portions of Racy's tip jar earnings had been buying new books for that often neglected section since she started working at The Blue Creek. Her private homage to one of the few places where she'd found solace and peace as a little girl.

"The Blue Creek has responded to the committee." Racy's voice remained deadpan. She hoped her face was the same. "We're not changing anything."

"Perhaps this list of concerned town folk on the committee will change your mind."

Racy didn't want to, but it was impossible not to look at the paper shoved under her nose. There were only a dozen or so names, but the last one caused her heart to freeze.

Sheriff Gage Steele.

He'd told her he didn't like her dancing on the bar, but she wasn't his wife. Not really. And he'd made it clear last night, while he'd enjoyed having sex with her in Vegas, he wasn't interested in a repeat performance now that they were home. She was sure he'd be on the phone with a new lawyer first thing Monday morning.

But this? She never thought he saw her girls in this way.

The burn of betrayal filled her gut and, what made matters worse, she had no idea why she felt so duped by him.

"I should have known better." Donna huffed, breaking into Racy's thoughts as she shoved her documents back into her folder. "The committee will be holding a hearing on this matter. I haven't lived in Destiny long, but that doesn't mean I don't know its history, or the history of certain citizens. A less than respectable upbringing and trashy life-style may lead you to believe this is acceptable—"

That's it. Tolerance level reached. Racy gestured to the door. "It's time for you to leave, Mrs. Pearson."

The woman turned and headed for the front entrance. Racy followed, making sure she didn't spout off to anyone else. Ric Murphy stood nearby and caught her eye. She nodded and he silently opened one of the double glass doors.

Racy waited until the woman stepped outside before she spoke. "I'll be sure to say hello to your husband the next time he drops by."

Mrs. Pearson faltered then continued to a luxury sedan in the parking lot. The direct hit felt good, but the humiliation over the woman's words burned deep.

It was a familiar feeling. A longtime companion from when she was a kid. It hadn't taken Racy long to figure out being labeled from the wrong side of the tracks wasn't completely about where she lived. Pretending she didn't care had worked for a while. And she'd tried hard to live up to the gossip during her teens and early twenties, her actions helping to mask the pain.

Now she was looking for respect and independence. Next month she'd have her business degree and she was going to offer to buy The Blue Creek from Max. But the fifty grand she'd won in Vegas, along with what she'd managed to save above and beyond paying for college, wasn't enough. She needed financing and she'd just made the wife of the bank president enemy number one.

Her weekend from hell was complete.

Gage leaned back in the aged leather chair and listened to the quiet hum as his computer shut down, mentally reviewing what he needed at the liquor store and deli, both planned stops on his way home.

Friday afternoon, one more meeting and his workweek was done. How being sheriff made him a member of the town's betterment committee he still didn't know, but the mayor, the school principal and a few other noted citizens were members, including his mother, so he considered it another one of his civic duties.

So far, the committee had done good things, like building the new playground at the elementary school and bringing in a couple of specialty stores to the downtown area.

A jazzy tune, either Dino or Frank, flowed through his closed office door. Alison, the sheriff department's office manager, had a thing for both crooners. At least she wasn't playing that damn Elvis CD again. Ever since Vegas, he couldn't listen to Elvis, and not just because the man—or an exceptional replica—had officiated at his and Racy's wedding.

Gage grabbed his coffee mug, took a swallow of the now cold liquid and grimaced. *Damn, he'd almost done it. Almost gone the whole afternoon without thinking about her.*

Since catching her spying on his workout last Sunday, he couldn't be in his sunroom without thinking about those sexy, bed-head curls, the open pajama top and the unzipped jeans that perfectly framed her flat stomach, the piercing in her navel glimmering in the sunlight.

And the glimmering desire in her eyes. For him.

Hell, it was impossible to be anywhere in his house without reliving the memories of last weekend. And if that buzzer on the washing machine hadn't gone off, they would've christened his new leather sofa with a repeat performance of wild sex.

Just like Vegas.

Only Gage didn't want that. Well, yeah he did. Who was he kidding? But ever since that amazing night, both in and out of bed, he'd begun to realize he wanted more. And he wanted it with the woman who happened to be his wife.

Too bad she didn't feel the same way.

He still wasn't sure how they'd gone from fighting about her brothers and career choices to being wrapped in each other's arms, but it felt good—damn good—to find out she remembered their time in Vegas. Previously she'd led him to believe she had no memory of the night's events. But now she'd admitted her memories, and things were a lot less clear-cut.

So instead of acting out any of the numerous fantasies in his head last Sunday morning, he'd gotten her and her dog out of his house as quickly as possible. Then he'd spent most of this past week either in the office or finishing up the lower level bathroom at his place in order to be ready for tonight.

Hell, he'd waited all week to be served with divorce papers. Real ones, this time, but nothing. Five days and not a word from Racy. No, that's not true.

He'd seen her on Wednesday, but only to take Jack home after finding the golden retriever on his front porch when he'd gotten off work. The dog had jumped into his Jeep, plopped on the passenger-side floor mat and seemed to enjoy the blast of hot air from the heater on his ragged, wet fur. Gage had no idea how the dog had gotten from Racy's place to his, but the mutt had seemed pretty happy to see him.

His owner didn't seemed so thrilled, though.

From her bedraggled appearance when she cracked open the door to allow the dog inside, he didn't know if she was sick or hungover. All he got was a weak thanks and then the door shut in his face.

"Am I interrupting?"

Gage looked up. "Hey, what are you doing here?"

"Surprised to see me?"

"After last night? Yeah."

His mom's still smooth cheeks flushed pink, making her look a decade younger than her fifty-five years. "Well, there's a first time for everything."

"Catching my mother steaming up windows on Make Out Mountain isn't one I'm looking forward to repeating."

Sandy Steele quickly stepped inside and closed the door behind her. "Shh!"

"Oh, now you're embarrassed?"

"You watch your tone, Gage Mitchell Steele." His mother's facial features shifted from flustered to stern in a heartbeat.

"Or what? You're going to stop talking to me like the rest of the family?"

Her fingers tightened on the quilted purse she clasped to her chest. "I came to walk with you to the betterment committee meeting." She turned to go. "I can see now that was a mistake."

Okay, he was a jerk.

Gage rose. "Mom, wait."

She didn't, and he had to grab his jacket and Stetson, and send Alison a quick wave as he rushed out the door. He hated that his brother and sisters were still giving him the cold shoulder, but that was no excuse for his behavior.

He slid to a stop to keep from crashing into his mother as she stood just outside the front door, depositing mail in a mailbox.

"Mom, I'm sorry."

She turned, a serene smile back on her face. "I know. I also know you don't normally snap at me. Has my dating Hank Jarvis really thrown you for such a loop?"

Gage slapped his Stetson on his head. "Can I admit hearing you even say the word *dating* bothers me?"

She tucked her hand in the crook of his arm. It had snowed twice in the last week, but the sun was shining this afternoon, and the sidewalk was clear. The town hall was in the next block just past the square. Gage followed his mother's lead past his Jeep, knowing she wanted to walk.

"It's been ten years since your father died, and Hank is a good man." She squeezed his arm. "He lost his true love over twenty-five years ago and we've been friends all our lives. Is it so wrong for us to want to spend time together?"

"Playing bingo is one thing. Making out in his truck is another."

Her soft laughter frosted the cold air. "Gina happens to think it's a great idea I'm doing more than decorating cakes and picking up after the twins."

Gage snorted. "Gina doesn't have the best judgment at the moment."

"She told me about your offer to help her find a job."

"Which she turned down flat."

"And how you tried to influence Max and Racy Dillon into firing her."

He busied himself with nodding hellos at passersby, using the few moments to control his reaction to *her* name. "You can't be happy with her working at The Blue Creek, either."

"Gina is an adult and can make her own career decisions. She dedicated herself to her education when she was just a child and I'd never seen her as excited as when she got the fellowship in London. But something caused her to walk away from that experience and return home."

"She hasn't told you what happened?"

His mother shook her head. "She keeps things buried deep, like your father. Like you. For now, I need to be satisfied she knows what she doesn't want."

"She doesn't want me meddling in her life."

"Oh, that's not true." She stopped and tugged on Gage's arm until he turned to look at her. "She loves her big brother, just as much as the twins do. Garrett was so excited when he got an early acceptance letter from Duke University yesterday, he couldn't wait to tell you."

Gage's heart swelled. His younger brother had dreamed

of being a Blue Devil since middle school. They'd toiled over his college application. To know he'd been accepted filled him with pride, but it was tinged with hurt that he'd heard the news secondhand.

"But he didn't call."

"Giselle reminded him they would be missing tonight's bonfire and skating party because they're still grounded."

"Thanks to me."

"And me. I agreed with grounding them for the month." Sandy started walking again. Gage fell into step beside her. "Don't worry, they'll come around. They're just chafing at your authority. You know, you've spent the last ten years being more like a dad to them than a brother. I was so lost when your father was killed. I relied on you to take care of them, of us."

"Mom, it was my choice to come home. I wanted to take care of my family."

"And you have, just like you've taken care of this town. But I think you're the one who needs to find some companionship, son." She moved to allow Gage to pull open the door to Destiny's Town Hall. "Fill that big, beautiful house of yours with a wife and lots of grandchildren for me to spoil."

A flood of heat filled him and he didn't know if it was his mother's words or stepping inside the building that had done it. He yanked down the zipper on his jacket as they entered the small meeting room. It didn't help.

A wife he had. He just didn't know for how long. Kids? Yeah, he'd always planned on having a handful, but he'd never found the right girl.

An image popped into his head.

His hands caressing a swollen belly, whispering nonsense over warm, tight skin as delicate fingers combed through his hair and caressed his neck. Looking up and finding a pair of chocolate-brown eyes shining with love and affection for him and their child.

"Racy Dillon."

Gage jerked from the fantasy when he heard Racy's name echo across the room. The fellow members of the committee sat around the table, in the midst of what looked like a heated argument.

"I'm telling you," Donna Pearson raised her voice to be heard over the din. "Miss Dillon and her dancers have to go. Her actions fall under the town's lewd and indecent bylaws. Sheriff Steele—" she caught Gage in a hard stare "—you're just the man to shut her down."

Chapter Eight

"What's your poison?"

"The usual." Devlin Murphy leaned against the bar and propped his arms on the smooth wood surface. He looked at Gage. "You're quiet tonight."

Gage popped the top off a cold root beer and handed it to his longtime friend. He watched Dev take a long swallow, knowing it was the closest the man had been to the real thing in four years. "You noticed, huh?"

"Despite the festivities." His friend waved the bottle at the center of the room, then lowered his voice. "You want to talk about it?"

Gage considered the offer. His and Dev's friendship had taken root in high school and never wavered despite the many times spent on opposite sides of a jail cell over the years.

When Dev had finally admitted to a drinking problem, Gage had been his ride to his AA meetings. When Gage had been ready to make his dream home a reality, Murphy Mountain Log Homes had been there for him.

Now, thanks to his friend's company, they were standing in the lower-level game room of said dream house. And at the moment, the room was filled with men, all here for the time-honored tradition known as a bachelor party.

Landon Cartwright had arrived an hour ago with a group that included the four cowboys who worked for him, his brother and his best friend, a lawyer from Texas who was also standing up for him at the wedding next weekend. Gage had greeted them with drinks and food and managed to look Hank Jarvis in the eye, oddly satisfied when the older man held his gaze.

"Did you hear me?" Dev asked.

"Yeah." Gage lowered his voice, staying just loud enough to be heard over the man-talk happening at the pool table. "I've got a lot on my mind."

Dev grabbed some chips, scooped up cheesy dip from a nearby bowl and tossed it all into his mouth. He chewed for a moment, then spoke. "Anything I can do?"

"Nah, it's nothing I can't handle."

He hoped.

The betterment committee meeting had gone longer than expected, with Donna Pearson ranting about Racy and the Blue Creek Belles. After a while, he wasn't sure if she was only interested in stopping the Belles or closing down the bar entirely. Either way, it was clear she wanted to get rid of Racy in the process.

He'd been surprised to learn about the letter the committee had sent to Max a month ago and of Donna's visit to The Blue Creek last Sunday. Both of which must have ticked off Racy to no end. From Donna's attitude, and knowing Racy like he did, he'd bet the fiery redhead's response had probably included a shot or two at the chairwoman's expense.

He'd tried to calm everyone, but Donna had a talent for whipping the members into an uproar, especially when she'd announced a hearing was scheduled for tomorrow with the town's selectmen and that a notice had been delivered to the bar's management.

Gage knew Max had gone to Florida for a couple of weeks of sun and golf. That left Racy to convince the town leaders her waitresses should be allowed to provide entertainment in their own way. He was sure she would arrive at the hearing full of attitude, and the end result would be one of the town's favorite distractions being outlawed.

A plan to fix this situation—for the town, the waitresses and for Racy—had formed inside his head as the meeting had ended. He'd been on his cell phone right up until his first guests had arrived. He hoped it would be enough.

"Is it the Dillon boys?"

Dev's question surprised him. "What makes you say that?"

"I saw Billy Joe the other day." Dev took another swallow of his drink. "I'm guessing from your reaction you know he and Justin are back in town. Billy Joe is doing repair work at Mason's Service Station, and my brother Ric said Justin is working in the kitchen at The Blue Creek."

Gage had learned about Billy Joe working for Racy's former father-in-law a few days ago. He wasn't surprised. Billy Joe and Racy's first husband had been friends and old man Mason was getting too far along in years to do much more than pump gas.

He also knew about Justin working with his sister from one of his deputy's daily reports. And no, he wasn't happy about it.

"Yeah, I know they're back." He tried to wash away the

bitter taste in his mouth with a long swallow. "They got out early on good behavior."

"Wonder how long that's gonna last. Are they staying with Racy?"

Gage shrugged. He hadn't seen either of them Wednesday when he'd returned Jack. "As long as they stay out of trouble, I don't care where they live."

Yeah, he almost sounded believable.

Dev raised an eyebrow and opened his mouth, but the jukebox in the corner came to life with a country song about cheating wives and love gone wrong. It mixed with the clanking of pool balls as a chorus of male groans filled the air.

"Dadgum! Who picked this song?" Willie called out. "Surely not the groom."

Gage saw Landon pretending to toss a dart at the aged cowboy and grinned.

"Good thing you got this thing rigged to play without coins, Sheriff," Willie continued as he pressed the reset button and punched in a new selection. "Can't have music disrespectin' the bride, not with the funeral—er, wedding just a week away."

"Is that any way to talk to a man who's about to walk the wedding plank?" Chase asked.

Willie grinned as he made his way to the bar. "Miss Maggie hog-tied your brother fair and square."

"That she did, but don't sentence me to the gallows before my time." Landon waved his left hand in the air. "There's no ring on this finger…yet."

The men laughed. Gage thought about the matching set of rings upstairs in his dresser drawer next to the invalid annulment papers.

"Hell's bells, you're a goner, Cartwright." Willie rapped a bony knuckle on the bar, signaling for a beer. "Our bachelor ranks are getting smaller every day. Other than Landon's fancy lawyer friend and Hank, the rest of us are members of the Not-Me, No-Way Club. Of course, I suspect those two other youngins at the pool table will fall for a pretty filly one day, too."

Gage's hand stilled on the icy bottle. He wasn't a member of that particular club. Not anymore, not since last summer.

To say he'd been shocked when Racy had stepped from a Vegas jewelry store and popped open the small velvet box would've put it mildly. In his wildest dream he'd never thought it possible—okay, maybe in his *wildest*. But he'd been speechless when Racy had slipped the smaller of the two diamond-studded bands on her ring finger and asked if he was interested in making things permanent. He'd managed to find his voice long enough to croak out a "sure," before she'd hauled his butt into a taxi headed for the Las Vegas licensing bureau.

Of course, no one here knew any of that. The question was how long he would stay married.

Whoa, is that what he wanted? To stay married?

"Oh, I don't know about that." Chase finished the dart game and reached for a pool cue. "It only takes the right lady to make a man change his mind about blessed bachelorhood."

"Come on, Gage. It's you and Dev against the Cartwright brothers." Landon joined his brother at the pool table. He picked up on Chase's previous comment. "You got someone in mind, little brother?"

"At my age?" Chase grinned. "I'm much too young to think about settling down."

"You mean too busy." Landon moved out of the way as Dev and Gage got their pool cues. "I'm surprised you haven't found any female companionship in Destiny in the week you've been here."

"Who says I haven't?"

"Miss Racy handpicked ya last weekend," Willie called from the bar, where he was now playing bartender. "If you ask me you were a fool to let that sweet gal slip through your fingers."

Gage's hand tightened on his pool stick. Chase's too handsome face lit up with a grin as he sent the triangle of balls scattering over the green felt.

"You might want to relax a bit." A deep voice flowed over Gage's shoulder. "You've got a while before you get in a shot. Chase is quite the pool shark."

He turned to find Bryce Powers, Landon's lawyer friend, standing behind him. When the man stepped away from the table to the windows, Gage followed. "He's quite the lady shark, too."

"Nah, Chase is just too pretty for his own good. Been that way since we were kids." Bryce drank from his glass. "For some reason, the ladies find him sweet and charming. The one thing I've never seen him do is poach another man's woman."

"What makes you think I care about his dating habits?" Gage leaned against the window frame, trying to shut out the conversation at the pool table.

"I notice things. Drives my wife nuts. Anyway, you're doing a good job of looking casual, but every time a certain lady's name is mentioned…"

The man's voice trailed off and his gaze dropped to where Gage still clutched the pool cue. He forced his fingers to relax without flexing them.

Were his feelings for Racy so obvious?

"Maggie told Maryann and me about the wedding arrangements. She said it felt strange to match you with your deputy, Leeann, I think her name was," Bryce continued, "but the only choice would be matching you and Miss Dillon."

"So?"

"So, Maggie seemed conflicted as to whether that would be a bad thing or not." Bryce smiled. "She's worried about you two sitting together at the reception, dancing together."

"And you paid attention during all this wedding talk?"

"What can I say? I'm a lawyer."

A damn good one if Landon's stories were to be believed. "You've been in this town less than twenty-four hours and you've got my love life figured out?"

"I didn't mention anyone's love life."

That's right, he hadn't.

Gage straightened and reached for his ice water on a nearby table. "Things between me and Racy are complicated. Been that way since we were teenagers."

"Please, no mention of teenagers." Dev interrupted as he joined them. "My older brother moved back to the family homestead with his three hoodlums and they're driving me nuts."

Silence reigned.

Dev's gaze shot between the two men. "Ah, did I interrupt something?"

"No." Gage quickly recovered. "Is it my shot?"

"Sorry, bud. Pool was never my game." Dev gestured over his shoulder. "Landon's shooting."

"I was just about to ask about the guitars." Bryce pointed at the wall. "Are those just for show or do you play?"

Gage looked at Bryce. Despite the smooth switch in topics, he did seem interested. "I play a little. The one on the far left is a vintage 1937 Gibson Century Hawaiian. It belonged to my grandfather. The middle one is a 1960 Gibson Hummingbird that was my dad's. The last one is mine."

"Let me guess. A Gibson?"

Gage smiled. "A '68 SJ Sunburst. My dad gave it to me on my sixteenth birthday."

Dev grinned. "We had a garage band in high school. Oh, man, we were bad. Gage was the only one with any musical talent."

"And yet you ended up in law enforcement?" Bryce asked.

"Music was just something to fool around with."

"Have you played lately?" Dev looked over at Bryce. "This guy used to have every Johnny Cash and Beatles song memorized."

"What? No Elvis?"

Dev barked out a gruff laugh. "Gage sing Elvis? No way!"

"Actually I sang an Elvis tune a few months ago." The words left Gage's mouth before he could stop them.

"You did?" Dev asked. "Why?"

Because Racy had asked him to.

After they'd returned from the licensing bureau, Racy got sidetracked by a high-stakes poker game. She'd won second place and was gloating over her winnings. Insisting she didn't want to be loved for her money, she'd threatened, in front of a gathering crowd, to call off their wedding until he'd proven he still wanted to marry her.

Kind of ironic since she'd been the one who'd proposed, but he hadn't considered that at the time. He'd only seen the challenge in her eyes, and had been determined to knock her right out of those sexy high heels.

Then three Elvises had walked by. A young rockabilly version, one clad in black leather from head to toe and the last decked out in one of those famous white jumpsuits. He'd borrowed a guitar from the leather-clad one, and right there on the casino floor, surrounded by slot machines and poker tables, he'd sung a song about wise men, fools and falling in love.

She was in his arms, her mouth fused to his, before the last note had faded.

"What did you sing?"

A scratching sound behind him saved Gage from an-swering Dev's question. He turned and saw Jack, Racy's golden retriever, his panting fogging the glass on the patio door.

"What the—" He let the dog inside. "Did the vet put a homing chip under your skin with the wrong address?" He dropped to one knee and scratched the dog's wet head. His reward was a sloppy kiss and full-body shakes that sent melting snow flying. "What are you doing here again?"

"Again?"

Gage turned to his guests. All wore a variety of quizzi-cal looks on their faces. Except for Bryce, whose mouth rose into a knowing grin.

"Sheriff." Dev's voice held a hint of laughter. "You want to explain why you and Miss Racy Dillon's beloved dog seem to be on such friendly terms?"

Racy stomped her feet in the ankle-deep snow, trying to return feeling to her cold toes. "Whose dumb idea was this?"

"The bride's."

"Hey, this is my day." Maggie laced her arm through Racy's and set off again trudging through the snow. "I'm allowed."

"To do what? Get our asses frozen off?" Racy side-stepped a fallen tree. "And your day isn't until Friday. What time is it?"

"It's almost twelve-thirty," Maryann said as she followed them. "Say, is this something you Northern girls do often?"

"Don't ask me." Leeann giggled from the back of the pack. "I was all for staying huddled around the marga-rita machine."

Racy groaned. It sucked being the only sober one.

Thanks to the notice she'd received this afternoon, she had to be at the town hall tomorrow—this morning, actually—in less than ten hours. Damn that Donna Pearson and everyone on her betterment committee. "Tell me again *why* we're doing this?"

"Because I want to know if they got strippers."

"Oh, please," Racy snorted. "They're probably drinking beer, playing cards and watching *SportsCenter.*"

"Or pornos," Leeann quipped.

"See?" Maggie huffed. "That's why we're checking."

"And we had to park on the highway and trudge through the woods?" Racy asked, thankful for the full moon and clear skies. "Can't we just walk up to the front door like normal people?"

"Name one normal woman in this bunch," Maggie said. "Sorry, Maryann."

"Don't apologize. I haven't had this much fun since my college days."

"Jeez, look at this place." Leeann's voice was filled with awe. "What does a single guy need all these rooms for?"

"Maybe he's not looking to remain single," Maggie said. "What do you think, Racy?"

"I think you've had one too many." Racy shoved her icy fingers into the deep pockets of her jacket.

"Hey, I was trying to keep up with Leeann. She drinks like a fish!"

"A little fish in an enormous, crowded pond…that sucks—whoops!"

Racy turned around in time to see Leeann save herself from falling into a snowbank by grabbing on to the closest tree.

"…sucks the life right out of you," she continued. "Trust me, ladies. It's better to be a little fishy in a little bowl. Better yet, a single fishy in one of those glass globes with the pretty rocks and a fake castle."

Racy leaned in to Maggie. "What is she talking about?"

"I don't know. She's been this way all night."

"I think this is the first time I've seen her drink since she's been back in town. And that's been—what? Over two years now?" Racy asked. "Do you really think we should take her to her boss's house like this?"

"Do you want to tell me why you have such an aversion to being at Castle Steele?" Maggie rounded the corner of the two-story log home with Racy on her heels. "You certainly made yourself at home here last weekend."

Racy pulled up short. "Wow, Lee's not the only one feeling no pain tonight."

The teasing glint left Maggie's eyes. "Racy, I'm sorry. I didn't mean that the way it sounded. And I know you believe otherwise, but I don't think Gage had anything to do with that complaint against the Belles."

Racy refused to accept that.

Or that she'd been crazy enough to blurt out her troubles with the town's betterment committee when Maggie had stopped by a few days ago to check on her. She'd blamed her lack of self-control on the cold medicine and Justin's amazing chicken soup, both of which helped her recover from a nasty bug. Not that she was back one hundred percent, but she was a long way from the pathetic soul she'd been during the week.

"I don't want to talk about Steele or the betterment committee."

"I know, but we're about to knock on his door."

The four of them now stood on a flagstone patio, cleared of snow and ice. Bright lights poured from the windows and muffled country rock came from the house.

"Don't you mean peer into his windows?" She resisted the urge to stomp her feet again, knowing the sound would echo in the night air. "Besides, he's on the committee. Enough said."

"Hey, lights!" Leeann staggered forward. "Let's sneak a peek!"

Racy grabbed an arm and held her back. "Oh, I think the bride should do the honors."

Maggie hesitated.

"Go on, future Mrs. Cartwright," Racy waved at the patio door. She couldn't see inside, but muted male laughter filled her ears. "We know your cowboys aren't in there, since Willie and the boys pulled in before we left the ranch. The only ones left should be your intended, his brother and Maryann's husband."

And their host.

Before Maggie took a step, the door opened.

"Okay, you crazy mutt, here you go." Gage's voice rang out as he stepped outside. "No rolling in the snow now that you're dry. And don't take off. Your mama will blame me if anything—"

"Jack!"

The golden retriever bounded across the patio, heading straight for Racy. She managed to keep Leeann and herself upright as her pup barked excited hellos that brought the rest of the men out of the house.

"What the—"

"What are you girls doing here?"

"Well, now the party's started!"

Landon wrapped Maggie in his arms and Bryce did the same to Maryann, leaving Racy to deal with a tipsy Leeann and a happy Jack.

"Hey, let me help."

Racy looked up to find Chase Cartwright next to her.

"Who do you want me to take?" He offered a smile. "The cop or the dog?"

"How did you know Leeann's a cop?"

Chase leaned closer and winked. "I have my sources."

"Well, I guess that depends," Racy quipped, "on which one you think you can handle."

Chase grabbed Jack's collar. "Jack and I have been watching the Celtics destroy my beloved Mavericks. We're buds now."

Racy released her hold on the dog's collar. "I don't know what he's doing here."

"He showed up about an hour ago."

The sharpness in Gage's voice caught Racy's attention. He stood at the doorway. Backlit, his face remained in shadows, but his stance—stiff shoulders and arms crossed over his chest—spoke volumes.

"Again? Why?"

"Yes, again and I don't know why. Perhaps you need a lock on your doggy door."

Abrupt and a smart-ass. Was he pissed because Jack seemed to have adopted his oversize Lincoln Log Cabin as his new doghouse?

"Why don't we take the party inside?" Gage stepped to one side and waved at the still open patio door. "You ladies look like you could use something to warm you up."

Leeann tugged free from Racy and followed the crowd inside, with wobbly steps. Racy moved in behind Chase and Jack, but a hand on her arm held her back.

"How did you get here?"

She didn't turn around. "In a car."

Gage sighed. "Racy."

"Look, this was the bride's idea, and the margaritas have been flowing since dinnertime. Leeann had already had two by the time I got to Maggie's place so I agreed to play chauffeur. I'll make sure she gets home safe and sound."

"I'm not an ogre. Leeann is off duty until Sunday. She's free to drink."

"Ogre, no," she whispered, stepping inside. "Jerk, yes."

"What did you say?"

Racy was saved from answering as they walked inside and Gage swung into hosting duties. He got everyone fresh drinks, mostly coffee and hot chocolate. She'd been right about who'd remained at the bachelor party, with one exception.

"Murph!" She returned Dev's bear hug. "What are you doing here?"

"Just enjoying some male bonding in Gage's man cave."

Racy stepped back and eyed her surroundings, taking in the man-size leather furniture positioned for perfect viewing of a wall-mounted flat-screen television. A Wurlitzer jukebox sat tucked in a corner near the bar, while a dartboard and pool table, both regulation size, completed the room. A room he'd insisted was empty a week ago.

"Yes, it's certainly a man cave," she said, turning back to Dev. "Not a feminine touch in sight."

"Well, it's a bachelor's home."

Technically, it wasn't. And it could use a plush throw blanket, a few sofa pillows and some artwork to really bring out the beauty of the log walls—

Racy halted that thought when Gage called Dev away to help with the drinks. She moved to the sofa and sat near Jack, who was stretched out contentedly by an oversize coffee table.

"Don't get too comfortable," she warned her pet. "You're banned from this place after tonight."

Jack heaved a deep sigh, closed his eyes and Racy swore the mutt's lips curved up into a grin.

"Extra hot, extra chocolate and enough whipped cream for three mugs."

Racy looked up. Gage was standing in front of her. She rose and took the mug, teetering with white foamy cream. "How did you—ah, Sherry's Diner. You know, you need to find yourself a hobby instead of memorizing my eating habits."

Gage leaned in closer. "I think I've got enough on my plate at the moment."

"Yeah, I bet you do." Racy tried to move back a step, as much as Jack's prone form would allow. "What with all those committees—"

"This is an amazing house." Maggie stood near the pool table. "Any chance we can see the rest of it?"

"I'm sure Gage would love to play tour guide," Landon said with a grin as he looked down at her, "as soon as you tell us why you crashed my party."

"Well, um…we wanted—that is, we figured—"

"We figured it would be more fun hanging with you boys," Maryann offered with a quick wink in Racy's direction.

"Yeah, the evening was shot after the male strippers left," Racy added, ignoring the gruff male laughter while returning Gage's direct stare over the rim of her mug.

"So, about that tour?" Maggie asked.

"Well, the place isn't a hundred percent complete, but if you want to see it." Gage put his mug on the coffee table. "Follow me, ladies."

The group headed for the doorway. Then Leeann turned around, having found her equilibrium. "You coming, Racy?"

"No, I'll stay with the guys. I fear I'm a bit too trashy to be walking among the hallowed halls of the sheriff's house."

Gage halted. He turned and glared at her. "What are you talking about?"

"Destiny's Betterment Committee."

Even in the dim light from the hallway, she saw a shadow pass over his dark eyes. She should let this go, but she couldn't. It still hurt to know what he thought of her and her work and that pissed her off even more.

He walked back past everyone until he stood in front of her again. "What about it?"

"You're a member."

"As town sheriff, it's my duty to be on all sorts of committees."

"Don't you know what they stand for?"

"Yeah, making the town a better place, hence the name. That includes upgrading the town gazebo, the new playground at the elementary school, making improvements to the fairgrounds—"

"Closing down The Blue Creek."

That gave him pause, and this time she saw the truth in his eyes. Anger flared hot and hard inside her chest. "You bastard! I saw the letter…I saw your name! It says by dancing on the bar, the girls are behaving improperly and immorally. Donna Pearson showed up herself last Sunday to tell me that we are no better than common strippers."

She planted her hands on her hips. "As if the Belles and I are responsible for sending every man in the county into a sexual frenzy, God forbid, and as a result bringing down the moral climate of the state. If you ask me, Donna Pearson could use a little sexual frenzy in her life."

"I didn't sign a letter."

"And now I have a hearing before the town selectmen—"

"I didn't sign any damn letter." Gage cut her off. "Not the original or the one they sent you today."

Chapter Nine

She could take her out. Right here. Right now. She wouldn't even need a running start to body slam Donna Pearson onto the meeting room's faded gray carpet. She'd have to slip off the stilettos, but that was okay, they were pinching her toes anyway.

Racy pulled in a deep breath through her nose and slowly released it through pursed lips. *Stay calm, it's almost over and you get the last word.*

Donna's sharp voice filled the room and echoed off the walls. Her censure of the Belles sounded more like a lecture from the pulpit on the sins of drinking, dancing and having a good time than a response to a community issue. And the community connection was Racy's ace in the hole.

She hoped.

Besides, her bar wasn't the only place in town to get a beer. There were a couple of other bars and a few restaurants, including the new steak house. Of course, none of them had dancing waitresses.

The seven men and women who made up the town's leaders sat side by side at a long table in front of her. The dozen or so members of the betterment committee occupied nearby chairs in the stuffy, small room.

And here she sat alone, with her leather portfolio in front of her, mentally willing herself not to sweat. Even the telephone that allowed Max to listen in from Florida was on the selectmen's table.

She'd already wowed them visually in her subdued basic black suit, Christian Louboutin knockoff stilettos, hair in a conservative French twist and demure makeup she hoped hid the results of only a few hours' sleep. And financially, with a detailed report of the economic impact The Blue Creek had on Destiny. Her compulsion to track every penny earned and spent since she had become manager had made it easy to pull the facts and figures together.

Forgetting the way she'd talked to Gage last night?

Not so easy.

After voicing his innocence in signing the letters in that low-timbred voice of his, he'd ushered her friends on to the promised tour of his house. Silence had filled the game room for a long moment until Dev had suggested he could make sure her friends got home okay.

Racy had jumped at his offer and after a quick apology for disturbing the party, she and Jack had left and headed straight for her office. She'd read an encouraging e-mail from Max, signing off on the report she'd sent earlier, then she'd pulled out the two betterment committee letters and read them again.

Gage hadn't signed them. Oh, his name was listed— along with the other members—but Donna's was the only actual signature on the two correspondences.

Damn, damn, damn!

She'd ignored the desire to call him despite the late hour. Instead, she'd arrived at the town hall early this morning determined to deliver an apology while the jolt from her first cup of coffee was still running through her veins.

Gage was nowhere to be found. Leeann had joined her, dressed in her official khaki uniform, not showing a hint of aftereffects from the night before. She'd been called into duty thanks to a three-car pileup on the highway that had required Gage's attention.

The meeting had been called to order and Racy had tucked away her frustration, refusing to think about why she cared if he was there or not. She'd been about to take her seat when the door had opened. Gage had stepped inside, his gaze moving quickly around the room. The double take he'd done when he'd caught sight of her set a fluttering through her insides, but then he'd clenched his jaw and pressed his lips into a frown as he took a seat next to his mother.

"Anything you'd like to say, Max?"

The deep voice of Selectman Roberts, a good friend and golf partner of Donna Pearson's husband, yanked Racy back to the present. Donna had returned to her seat, hands folded primly on her lap.

"Nope." Max's voice rose from the speakerphone. "I'll let my manager speak for The Blue Creek."

"Miss Dillon?"

She checked her watch. They'd been at it for almost three hours. It was close to lunchtime and people were drooping. Short and sweet was the way to go. She rose, took a breath and waited until she had everyone's eyes on her.

Including Donna's. And Gage's.

"There isn't too much more I want to add. As you saw in my financial report, The Blue Creek is a viable business, supporting a number of townspeople as employees as well as other businesses in Destiny with its steady flow of out-of-town customers. And part of that is because of the entertainment we provide, everything from up-and-coming country bands to the Blue Creek Belles. As I already told the betterment committee, being a Belle is strictly voluntary, not a condition of employment, and the security team is always in place to ensure the safety of both the waitresses and the customers.

"And it's those waitresses, the rest of the staff and the town's citizens, many of whom have worked their way through college by being employed at The Blue Creek, which make it a success. Present company included, like myself and Selectman Anderson, who waitressed at the Creek twenty years ago. As you know, Mrs. Anderson divides her time between her law practice and being a town selectman."

The older woman, still as petite and curvy as she was in the group staff photos that lined Max's office, smiled at her.

"We currently have numerous students on staff, but also mothers and fathers looking to make ends meet and pay the bills. Sherri Hart is one of my Belles. With three kids at home she needs to subsidize her husband's monthly government checks, thanks to his sacrifice while serving in the National Guard."

As she spoke, Racy realized she was fighting for more than just her dancers. If Donna Pearson won this battle it would only be a matter of time before she tried to close down the bar altogether. That wasn't going to happen.

The Blue Creek had been her safe haven over the years, a place she could count on when the rest of her world was spinning out of control. She'd started working as a waitress just months before her first husband had died, and here she was, eight years later, only a loan agreement away from offering to buy the place and make it truly her own.

She'd be damned if anyone would take it away from her.

"But the most important thing The Blue Creek brings to this community is its connection to Destiny's history. On the land where the current building stands, the original Blue Creek Saloon was founded in 1878. The brick wall behind the main bar is the only part of that building still with us. Before Wyoming was a state, when Destiny wasn't much more than a stop on the road, there was The Blue Creek. It was here before the first school, the first church, the bank or the sheriff's office."

She glanced at Gage. When the corner of his mouth lifted into a half grin, she tore her gaze away and focused again on the men and women at the center table. "The Blue Creek Saloon deserves to stay in its present form and continue to be run by the people who have made it the success it is today. Thank you."

Racy sat, wanting desperately to draw in a deep, cleansing breath. She settled instead for a quick prayer.

"It's almost lunchtime." Selectman Roberts looked at his watch, "And the fact is we're in a special session, so I'm calling for an immediate vote. Please remember, this is purely for approving an ordinance against the type of dancing performed by select employees at The Blue Creek Saloon, nothing more. A 'for' will signify approval of the ordinance, a 'nay' will be a vote against and the dancing will remain."

Donna opened her mouth to protest, but was quickly silenced. Racy sat perched on the edge of her seat and tried to give off an air of calm.

Roberts voted against allowing the dancing, as did the gentleman next to him, also a close friend of Donna's husband.

You knew that was going to happen. Don't panic.

Five more votes and she needed four of them.

Nancy Anderson was next and she offered Racy a quick

wink and voted in favor of the Belles. Next was the owner of The Destiny Inn, a bed-and-breakfast located in a restored Victorian, who spoke of enjoying his first beer at The Blue Creek after returning home from serving in Vietnam. He also voted her way.

Two for, two against.

The next vote went against the Belles and the smirk on Donna's lips seemed to rise right up into her eyes. Racy lifted her chin and returned her stare as the only other woman on the selectmen board voted for the dancing while invoking the Bill of Rights. Racy had no idea which amendment covered her girls, but she was thankful for the support.

Donna looked away.

Three for, three against.

The final and deciding vote was going to come from local businessman Travis Clay, whose family history went back to the first settlers of Destiny. He owned a few businesses, including a Western-wear store next to The Blue Creek. Racy couldn't say he was a regular in the bar, but he did come in often enough with people she assumed were business associates.

Of course, she did have a somewhat sordid history with his twin daughters, who had graduated high school with her. The Clay sisters had run with the popular crowd, hence the unpleasantness when they'd taken a few too many pokes at Racy's expense. She'd responded with a well-played prank, but that was years ago.

Travis, his eyes on Racy as he leaned forward and laced his fingers together, paused before he spoke.

"Nay."

A muted cheer came from outside the meeting room doors. It set Selectman Roberts in action and he announced the final vote and banged his gavel, ending the meeting.

She'd won.

She'd actually done it.

Racy grinned, keeping her composure in check as fireworks of pride and joy erupted inside of her. She stood and gathered her paperwork. A quick glance at Donna found her surrounded by a few committee members. Her stiff posture and the high-and-mighty air hadn't changed at all.

"Congratulations, Miss Dillon."

Racy turned to find Sandy Steele at her table. Her breath caught in her throat and she had to force herself not to look around for Gage. "T-thank you, Mrs. Steele."

"I want you to know many of the committee members were surprised by Donna's actions. We didn't learn of her letters until the meeting yesterday." Gage's mother spoke as she buttoned her winter coat. "Donna has worked wonders for the town. Perhaps her successes and the committee's willingness to follow her lead—"

Sandy Steele cut off her own words and smiled. Her blue eyes, the same ones inherited by her son, sparkled. "I didn't mean to rattle on, just know that many of us are glad the vote went your way."

Gage headed toward Racy and his mother, but walked by without a glance in their direction. Racy tried to squelch her disappointment and kept her gaze from following him from the room. What did she expect? So, okay he didn't sign the letters, but he still wasn't happy about his sister working at her bar.

Racy grabbed her purse and coat from the back of the chair. "Thank you. It's nice to know not everyone shares Donna's opinion."

Reading Racy's mind, Sandy touched her arm. "Gage is having a hard time remembering his little sister is now an adult. He's protective of those he loves and feels responsible for, and that often includes the citizens of Destiny."

The warmth of the older woman's hand felt good on

Racy's skin. She'd tried over the years to convince herself growing up without a mother wasn't such a terrible thing, but moments like this made her mindful of what she'd missed.

She looked at the simple gold band on Sandy's hand, and realized she was talking with the woman who was legally her mother-in-law.

A lump lodged in her throat.

That made Gina her sister-in-law. And the twins, Garrett and Giselle—Garrett, the spitting image of his father and older brother, and Giselle, who'd served her this morning at the doughnut shop—were family, too.

No, they weren't. She and Gage weren't married. Not really.

She cleared her throat to rid it of the tightness and said goodbye. After speaking to as many selectmen as she could, especially those who'd voted her way, she shared a quick word with Max on the phone. Joy at her boss's praise bubbled inside her and, when she left the room, the crowd outside caused her to stop as another cheer filled the air.

"What's going on?"

Faithful customers gathered around as she accepted hugs and congratulations from many of her staff. Gina was the last to step forward. She gave her a quick squeeze and then handed over a single yellow rose, a small card attached to its stem with a ribbon. "Way to go, boss. This is for you."

"Thank you." Racy took the rose.

"We wanted to be here to support you. And the rose isn't from me. Justin was skulking around for a while, but had to head back to the bar to get ready for the lunch crowd."

Skulking? Yes, that described her brother's behavior of late. They'd hardly spoken in the last week, except when it was job related.

Racy peeked at the card.

Knock 'em dead, kid! Love, Justin

She smiled and breathed in the flower's sweet fragrance. Justin might be spending the majority of his time being seen-but-not-heard, but he was working hard to stay on the straight and narrow.

"Thanks for coming, everyone. I appreciate it more than you know." Racy caught sight of Gage standing at the back exit of the building, his cream-colored cowboy hat cradled in his hands. "I look forward to seeing you all at The Blue Creek real soon."

The crowd started to scatter. This was her chance. She walked toward Gage. His eyes narrowed as she got closer, but she kept going until they stood toe to toe.

"I owe you an apology."

She kept her voice low, even though they stood apart from everyone. The ambivalence in his eyes had her worried he might walk away, and she was determined to get this over with.

"You were right," she continued. "Your signature wasn't on the letters. So go ahead. Have at it. Cut me up one side and down the other, but I've got to tell you, I'm riding such a high from winning there is nothing you can say to bring me down."

"I accept."

"Huh?"

"Your apology." Gage put on his Stetson. "I accept."

"Oh."

"Isn't there something you want to say in return?"

Let's get naked? Racy clamped her jaw shut until she was sure the words wouldn't pop out of her mouth. "Such as?"

"How about, thank you?"

"Thank you?"

Gage's gaze traveled the length of her body before he focused on her face again. His eyes now shined with a friendly gleam. "You look amazing."

Heat filled her face. Damn, she was too old to be blushing. "Thank you."

He waved the bound packet of paper he held rolled in his hand. "This report was amazing."

Her smile grew. "Thank you."

"Your speech was amazing."

"Gage, stop."

A smile pulled at one corner of his mouth. "Ah, not the right two words."

She didn't speak and he offered a raised eyebrow. She relented. "Thank you."

He hesitated, then took a step forward, closing the already narrow gap between them. "You working tonight?"

Racy nodded, heart racing, trying to disregard the crisp, clean scent that clung to his clothes and skin. "I'm headed to the bar from here."

"What about tomorrow?"

Why was he asking? Surely he couldn't… "Spending the day in Cheyenne with the girls. We've got a final fitting for our bridesmaids' dresses and other wedding stuff."

"Tomorrow night?"

She shook her head, ignoring the thrill at his persistence. "I should be home around dinnertime. I've got some last-minute studying for my finals next week."

"And your brothers won't get in the way of that?"

Her heart thumped so hard she swore it was visible beneath her suit jacket. Maybe she should've worn something more than bright purple lace beneath it, but hell, this morning she'd needed the mental oomph that she'd got from her favorite lingerie. "Ah, no, Billy Joe and Justin aren't staying with me anymore."

"They're not?"

"Billy Joe moved into one of the apartments over Mason's Garage. You know he's working there, right?"

Gage nodded and his eyes intensified to a dark blue. She didn't know what that meant, but took his silence as a sign to continue.

"Justin is staying at The Blue Creek. He's converting a few of the storage areas on the second floor into an apartment."

The admiration in those blue eyes changed to suspicion. "And Max is okay with that?"

Racy bristled. "No, but I figured it was okay to allow an ex-con to be less than a hundred feet from the safe without consulting Max."

"Forget I said that." His fingers reached out to lightly touch her hand. "How about I get some takeout and come over? We can—" The radio on his hip squawked, cutting him off. He grabbed it and pressed a button. "Steele here."

"Sheriff, you're needed out at MacIntire's place."

"What's going on?"

"The bonfire from last night's senior-class party has been reignited." Alison's clear voice came over the radio. "Jesse MacIntire caught his boy and a few others out by his pond. And I hate to say it, boss, but one of them is—"

"Garrett," Gage interrupted. "Is the fire under control?"

"Jesse said it's out, but the boys were tearing apart an old shack to use for firewood."

"I'm on my way."

Racy bit her lip to keep from smiling at the resigned look on Gage's face. "You know, maybe your brother needs something to keep him busy during his free time."

"With football season over, he does seem to have a lot of it on his hands."

"He could take some of that energy and put it toward the after-hours program at the elementary school." Racy offered the first idea that popped into her head. "I'm sure those kids look up to the high school players. They'd get a kick out of having them act as mentors."

"That might be a good idea. He could recruit some of his fellow pranksters." Gage backed up toward the door. "I've got to run, but I'll call you later?"

He paused, and Racy realized he was waiting for her to reply. She couldn't help herself. "Sure."

The smile he gave her was warm and genuine and it heated her right down to her toes. He was going to call her.

To firm up plans. Just like a real date.

Yee-haw!

She watched him disappear out the door, then tucked the rose inside her bag and set it on the floor to tug on her jacket. Spotting a water fountain, she ducked down the back hall for a drink. She pressed the button, the water cold on her lips when she heard Travis Clay's voice.

"Yep, that pretty little lady made quite a speech."

"I agree with you one hundred percent."

Racy heard the other male voice reply and recognized it as Daniel Gates's, the owner of The Destiny Inn. Pride filled her chest at their words. Damn straight she'd done a good job!

"You know," Travis continued, "I would've voted Miss Dillon's way even if the sheriff hadn't talked to me first."

Racy froze. Her thumb slipped and the stream of water trickled to a stop.

What did he just say?

"So, Gage got a hold of you, too?" Daniel said. "His call came just as I was opening that darn fool letter from the committee yesterday afternoon. Heck, what do I care if a bunch of girls want to shake their butts for a crowd?"

Travis guffawed. "I admit I enjoy watching them Belles myself from time to time, but it was good to listen to the man be persuasive anyway."

"What did the good sheriff promise you?"

"Oh, I vowed to keep that a secret. What about you…"

The voices faded as the back door opened and closed

again. Racy stood motionless, shock nailing her feet to the floor.

She couldn't believe it. Gage had tried to sway the vote before the meeting? Her detailed report, her passionate and genuine love for her business hadn't made any difference. He'd already convinced them to vote her way for their own selfish reasons, whatever they were.

She realized she should be grateful to Gage. So why was she so damn mad at him instead?

Chapter Ten

Damn, he hoped his tie was straight.

Gage entered through the side door and slipped into the empty space at the front of the candlelit church as the music started. He accepted a smile from Bryce, ignored Chase's scowl and returned Landon's wink. All members of the Cartwright-Stevens wedding party were finally present and accounted for.

Thanks to spending the last two days in Cheyenne testifying at a trial and getting a flat tire on the way home, Gage had only minutes to wash up at his office, change into his tux and head to the church.

The music swelled and Anna, Maggie's daughter from her first marriage, entered the doorway and started down the aisle. She walked slowly, taking her flower girl duties seriously. With every step, she dropped deep red rose petals that matched the color of her dress. Maryann followed, her gaze centered on her husband, who stood at Gage's right.

Leeann appeared next. She wore the formal wear with an easy elegance, which surprised him as he rarely saw her in anything but a uniform or jeans. He watched her until she was halfway down the aisle, but then his breath caught and his attention was drawn to the woman standing in the doorway.

Racy.

Despite the so-called plans they'd made after the hearing, it was the first time he'd seen her in almost a week. Resentment and desire pinged around inside him like a vintage pinball machine as he took in the deep red dress that clung to her curves and the mass of curls piled high on her head. Her peaches-and-cream skin glowed along with her smile as she followed Leeann and Maryann, her gaze moving over the crowded pews and the men standing with him at the altar.

Then her gaze locked with his.

Her chocolate-brown eyes widened for a moment, almost as if she was surprised to see him. He tried to hold her gaze, but she looked away. Her smile remained, but the joy behind it dimmed. She took her place next to Leeann, right in his sights, but she stubbornly refused to glance his way.

What the hell was going on?

She'd blown off their dinner plans last weekend and he was clueless as to why. Calls had gone unreturned and when he'd tried to see her in person…

Everyone rose as the bride entered, but Gage couldn't stop his gaze from going back to Racy. He tried to will her to look at him, but she trained her gaze on Maggie, a wistful look on her face. Maggie arrived at the altar and handed her flowers to Racy, who offered her a quick wink.

The solemn words of the wedding service started. He was instantly taken back to that moment in Vegas when he and Racy had exchanged vows, complete with strangers for witnesses and Elvis as the preacher. Not much of a ceremony and certainly not what every little girl dreamed of, but still special. The words they had spoken were the same Maggie and Landon repeated to each other as they exchanged rings. He found the fingers on his left hand tingling and rubbed at the sensation, then saw Racy mirror his movements, even with two bunches of flowers in her grasp.

The bride and groom kissed and the church erupted in applause. Anna ran from the front pew to join her mother and new stepfather. A crowd gathered, with hugs, kisses and well-wishes for the happy couple.

Now was his chance.

He slipped around the back of the crowd, stepped on the altar, then headed straight for Racy. She'd just handed Maggie's flowers back to her and he grabbed her hand.

"Racy, wait."

The coldness of her skin surprised him, but not as much as the shock in her eyes when she realized who held her. She tugged free and turned away.

Gage moved in behind her, his mouth at her ear, so the surrounding crowd couldn't overhear them. "What the hell is going on?"

She jerked her head to the side and hissed, "Shh!"

"Don't *shh* me. I want to know—"

She slid between Leeann and Nana B., Maggie's grand-mother, as the bride and groom started up the aisle. The crowd fell in behind them, Gage included. Those were far from the last words between them.

Hours later, he headed for the bar in the back room of The Painted Lady, the local bed-and-breakfast inn Maggie and Landon had chosen for their wedding reception, finally accepting the truth.

Racy was avoiding him.

The idea had popped into his head more than once over

the last week, but he'd made excuses, refusing to give credence to the notion. He'd waited until the pictures were done and the dinner had started before trying to get close to her again, but her covert moves made sure there were always plenty of people between them. After the first few tries, he got the message.

Loud and clear.

The bride and groom had left for their honeymoon almost an hour ago and the reception was winding down. The disc jockey packed up and most of the guests were either heading home or to the inn's pub to continue the party. He wasn't in a party mood. What he needed was a healthy splash of whiskey. He paid for the drink and walked to one of the arched floor-to-ceiling windows to stare into the dark night.

This wasn't like the fiery redhead. The woman he knew dealt with whatever was bugging her head-on, full force, with no apologies. Not this time. And that caused an uneasy feeling in his gut.

He lifted his glass for another taste, swallowed and then stilled, catching Racy's warped reflection in the window. He turned, knowing instinctively he was her intended target. Her gaze landed on him and she paused. Gone was the social butterfly he'd watched flirt, laugh and dance with everyone else tonight. Everyone but him. Her bare shoulders were stiff, her eyes devoid of emotion as she started toward him.

"We need to talk."

Her voice was low, the tone brittle. Makeup played up her perfect features, smoky dark eyes and shiny pink lips, but it was like she wore a mask for all the feeling he saw there.

"Now's a good time for you?" Gage tightened his grip on his glass. "I thought we were going to talk last week. I tried to reach you twice at the bar, but Justin intercepted my calls."

"I was working."

"I called Sunday about dinner. All I got was your machine."

She lifted her chin, and her eyes, direct and probing, met his. "I was studying. I told you I had finals."

Her clipped answers were getting on his nerves.

"Look, I don't know what's going on." Gage pulled in a deep breath and her familiar vanilla-lime scent filled his head. "Last week we—"

"I don't want to talk about last week."

"What do you want to talk about?"

She yanked a long white envelope from the slim, beaded purse in her hand and held it out to him. "Here."

"What's that?"

"Divorce papers."

The air disappeared from his lungs and bright spots danced in front of his eyes. His skin felt like it was on fire despite the winter chill that seeped through the antique window. Of all the things he'd expected her to say, that wasn't it.

She shook the envelope, her knuckles pale. "Take it."

"How—" He gulped a breath of much-needed air. "When—"

"Last week. I went to see a lawyer when I was in Laramie."

He focused on the corner of the envelope, recognizing the name of the law firm. "One of the most prestigious."

Racy offered an unladylike snort. "I wanted to make sure this time we did it right. You know, with a *real* lawyer?"

Gage stared at the woman in front of him. As beautiful as ever, but without the flushed-with-victory euphoria that had shined from her after the hearing.

When he'd entered the meeting room, he'd been shocked at the sight of her in a dark suit, her hair pulled back in a smooth style. Gone was the wild, girl-from-the-wrong-side-of-the-tracks bartender and in her place had stood a confident professional. And when they'd talked afterward, she'd been on top of the world. It'd taken all his strength not to pull her into his arms and cover her mouth with his. He'd settled instead for a date, sort of. She'd been receptive to the idea of getting together. He'd seen it in her eyes.

"I don't understand. What happened?"

"What's there to understand? W-we screwed up, twice, and it's time to get out of this mess." Her voice shook as she flung her arms wide. "And that's what this is, a mess, not a marriage. What Maggie and Landon have? That's real. They have love and commitment, passion and caring. Two people who've worked through the adversity of their pasts to believe and trust—"

She bit hard at her lip, cutting off her words and dropped her hands. A deep, shuddering breath had her closing her eyes. "Don't you see? This—this sham between us…it's nothing. It's not real to anyone but the law. So here, sign it."

Frozen by the fervor of her impassioned words, it took a hard swallow before he trusted his voice. "Racy—"

"Just sign it, Gage…please."

It was the "please" that got to him. "Fine."

He placed his glass on the table and took the envelope. Holding it, he patted the outside of his tuxedo jacket. "I—ah, I don't have a pen on me."

Racy yanked open her purse as he withdrew the paper-work from the envelope.

He shouldn't be shocked, not really. How had he expected this—whatever this was between the two of them—to end? They couldn't manage a simple dinner date. Did he really think their spur-of-the-moment marriage would transform into the real thing just because dumb luck found him still legally bound to the one woman he'd always wanted?

He unfolded the papers, mentally steering himself for the words.

Buyout Proposal?

After a quick scan of the first few paragraphs, confusion gave way to awareness. He looked up. "You're trying to buy The Blue Creek?"

Racy stilled, a pen in her outstretched hand. "What?"

"This says you're offering Max a buyout, contingent on loan approval and a deposit of—" Gage paused and checked the dollar figure listed again. "Is that what you're spending your Vegas winnings on?"

Racy yanked the papers from his hand. "That is none of your business." She turned and stalked away. "Damn, how could I be so stupid! You'd think at least once I could do something without screwing it up, but no, this is classic me all the way…"

Her words faded as she disappeared into the ballroom.

"Hey, wait!" Gage called out, following her. He dodged the staff clearing away soiled linens and folding tables, and saw her exit the other side of the room into the large, open foyer that served as the inn's lobby.

Racy marched past the check-in counter and stopped at the single antique elevator. She jammed her finger on the up button and spun around. "No, you wait. Right here. I've got the correct paperwork in my room."

The doors creaked open and she stepped inside.

"Room?" Gage reached the elevator just as the door slid closed again. "What room?"

"The bridal suite."

He spun around to find Leeann standing behind him. "Excuse me?"

"She's heading to the suite Maggie reserved," Leeann said.

"Maggie and Landon were supposed to stay here tonight, but the groom surprised her with a trip to the Caribbean."

"So why is Racy up there?" With one hand behind his back, he pressed the elevator button.

If she thought he was just going to scrawl his name on some paperwork and walk out of here, she had another think coming. Thank God she'd given him the wrong document and he had a minute to collect his thoughts.

Leeann crossed her arms over her chest. "Maggie told her to use the room since it was paid for. I was just about to go up and see if she wanted some company, since she seemed a little edgy, at least for Racy's standards, when I spotted—" She paused, uncertainty crossing her face. "Can I say something? I mean to my friend, Gage, and not to my boss, the sheriff?"

Gage hesitated, then nodded.

"I don't know what's going on between you two." She drew in a deep breath and slowly let it out. "Personally, I always thought Racy had little use for you, despite what happened in high school."

Chagrin filled him at the old memories that seemed to be foremost in his mind recently. "What did she tell you?"

"That's something between girlfriends." She waved away his interruption and continued. "I was gone for a number of years, years that were hard on her. Of course, her whole life has been one of adversity, but she finally seemed to be in a good place this past summer. Until Vegas."

Leeann took a step closer and lowered her voice, even though no one else was in the lobby. "Maggie believes there's something Racy's not telling us. You and she in the same city, over the same weekend? Could be nothing. But if it's more—if you two are—well, she deserves to be treated like a queen, you know?"

It was the longest he'd heard his deputy speak since her

acceptance speech when she was crowned Miss Indian Paintbrush back in high school. But he knew behind her warning was the warmth of a lifelong friendship.

"Racy's got a good friend in you."

Leeann's smile was forced. "That elevator is slower than molasses. If you want to catch her before she gets back down here, you might want to take the stairs. It's the only room on the fourth floor."

Gage eyed the majestic staircase that rose from the center of the foyer before it turned a hard left and disappeared from sight. He'd already pushed the button calling the elevator back, so he should have time. Or he might meet her on the wide oak stairs.

He turned back to say something to Leeann, but all he saw was the closing of the ornate cut-glass doors that led to the inn's covered porch.

Moments later, he was halfway up the stairs, his mind churning over what had happened between him and Racy earlier. She had some explaining to do. About everything. From why she'd blown him off last week to trying to buy the bar. And he wasn't signing a damn thing until he got some answers.

He reached the top floor and jogged past the elevator. No Racy. At the door displaying a brass plate that read Bridal Suite, he paused to catch his breath and prayed he hadn't missed her. Then he heard not-so-feminine cursing, a yelp of surprise and a crashing sound. He pushed open the unlatched door, rushed inside and was greeted with a loud popping sound before a spray of cold liquid hit him square in the chest.

He put one hand up to ward off the rush and it splattered into his face. Damn, that stung. He shook his head, trying to clear his eyes. "Racy! What the hell—are you okay?"

"Yes, I'm fine."

He wiped away the moisture. "What happened?"

Racy lay sprawled in front of the lit fireplace with an overturned champagne bucket nearby and ice cubes scattered everywhere. "I tripped over the bucket. What does it look like?"

He watched her struggle to her feet. Her dress tangled around her legs, revealing strappy shoes and toes painted a matching shade of deep red. Then she bent over to right the bucket and his breath evaporated. The low cut of her dress barely held back her breasts.

He scrubbed both hands over his face. Partially to get rid of the last of the liquid, and partially to block the tempting image in front of him. Too late. She bent again, now reaching for ice cubes. His body responded, hard and fast.

She tossed a few handfuls of ice into the bucket and kicked the rest into the blazing fire. "What a waste. And that was the good stuff—what in the hell are you doing?"

Gage stopped mid-peel, his tuxedo jacket hanging from his arms. He looked up to find Racy staring at him. He continued to tug and placed the jacket on the back of a wing chair. "Trying to save what I can of this rented tux."

"No one told you to strip. And what are you doing up here?"

He tugged at his drenched cotton shirt. "We need to talk. Do you think I could get a towel or something?"

Racy stared at him for a long moment. She then heaved a deep sigh and marched past him, slamming closed the door he'd left open when he'd charged in. He exhaled sharply as she disappeared through another doorway. The bathroom, he guessed.

His gaze moved around the room. Only one way in and lots of windows. It looked like at one time it could've been two rooms, but now was one large space. Matching chairs flanked the fireplace and a huge four-poster bed, piled high with flowery bedding and at least a dozen pillows, took up the far wall.

He recognized the warm Old World French country style thanks to his mom, who'd redecorated the family's home over the last few years. She preferred bright reds, greens and black, while this room, from the wallpaper to the fresh flowers, was done in soft colors and full of charm and romance. Tailor-made for a new bride and groom who wanted to make their special day unforgettable.

He closed his eyes, but the image came anyway.

Racy, dressed in white lace. Soft, flowing and completely transparent in the candlelight. She emerged from the bathroom, red curls falling in soft waves over her shoulders, concealing the tiny silk ties that held the nightie together. She walked toward him, a matching set of champagne glasses in her hands, a large diamond ring, his ring, sparkling on her finger.

Standing in front of him, a sweet smile on her face, she offered him a glass. He ignored it and instead pulled her into his arms, giving one of those silk ties an easy tug. A cloud of lace floated to the ground as he—

A soft thud in the face ended the fantasy. He caught the bath towel before it fell to the floor.

"There's your towel."

Racy stood across the room. She'd changed out of her dress, but instead of silk and lace, she wore pajamas in the same style he'd given her the night she'd stayed at his place. Only this time she wore the bottoms, too. And hers were pink.

Okay, the fantasy had to change a bit, but he was up for that. Very up.

"You changed." His words came out in a rough whisper as he rubbed the towel over his soggy shirt. It didn't help. He yanked the shirt from his pants and unbuttoned it.

"M-my dress got wet, too." Racy's gaze traveled the

length of him before she crossed her arms over her chest and looked away. "And the double-sided tape that kept my boobs from falling out was starting to itch."

He didn't know how to respond to that so he remained silent, noticing she kept her gaze focused on the fire as he rubbed the towel over his bare chest. Her hair remained piled on top of her head and she still wore the dangling earrings from the wedding. He glanced down. Her shoes were gone and her bare toes curled into the carpet.

Damn! Sexy and sweet at the same time.

His gaze traveled upward as he walked toward her. "Are those Eiffel Towers you're wearing?"

"Not that it's any of your business—" she looked at him again "—but Maggie, Leeann and I exchanged pajamas for our last birthdays."

"And your dream destination is Paris."

Her mouth dropped open. "How'd you know?"

He took a step closer, the towel partially obscuring his view as he rubbed at his hair. "You told me in Vegas."

"I did not."

"Yes, you did." One more step and he was directly in front of her. He dropped the towel. He wanted to see her face. "Right after I fished you out of the fountain at that hotel with the fake Eiffel Tower."

The memory was as clear as if it had happened yesterday.

She'd slipped off her high heels and was calf-deep in water before he'd realized what she was doing. He'd gone in after her, cowboy boots and all, when they'd caught the attention of a security guard. He'd carried her in his arms the six blocks back to their hotel before she'd insisted on—

"I don't remember."

Her soft words caused the recall to fade. He couldn't tell if she was lying or not. "But you do remem—"

"What I remember is you dropping the bomb about our

invalid annulment two weeks ago." She cut him off as she pushed past, hurried to the desk and flipped through a manila folder.

Gage draped the towel back over his head to muffle his groan of frustration. Back to square one. Less than square one, if Racy had her way.

"Where'd you get the money to have that paperwork drawn up, anyway?" He latched on to the first thought that came into his head. "That firm charges a bundle."

"None of your business."

He tossed the towel to the floor and crossed the room. Grabbing her by the arm, he spun her around. "Racy—"

"Take your hands off me."

Gage released her, but braced his arms on the desk, trapping her with his body. "You need to explain and you need to do it now."

"I don't have to do anything—"

"Then you can go back to your fancy lawyer and drop a large retainer on him because your simple and quiet divorce is going to get loud and ugly."

Her eyes widened. "You wouldn't do that!"

He leaned in closer. "And I never thought you'd blow me off last Sunday, but I guess both of us can be wrong, huh?"

"Now, there's an understatement."

"Enough of the riddles and innuendos. For someone who prides herself on being direct, you certainly seem to enjoy dancing in circles when it comes to talking to me."

"You want direct?"

"Yes."

"Fine. What did you promise Travis and Daniel?" She jabbed him in the chest with a pointed finger. "Are you going to look the other way when it comes to zoning laws? Or maybe you gave them each a get-out-of-jail-free card?"

Gage jerked back. "What are you talking about?"

"I heard them! Last Saturday, after the meeting, I heard them talking about your phone call and your promises…" Her voice faltered and she swallowed hard before continuing. "I even followed them outside and what did I find? Three good ol' boys sharing handshakes and smiles."

Realization hit him as cold as that champagne shower. "I can explain."

She squared her shoulders and crossed her arms under her breasts. "Oh, I just bet you can."

He forced himself not to look at the deep cleavage her move created as the top button on her pajama top popped open. Flashes of her half dressed, buttons undone on another pajama top, filled his head. He willed the image away. "Yes, I spoke with Travis and Dan about your hearing. I was worried. I know how much the bar means to you—"

"So you didn't trust me to get the job done and tried to sway the voting with bribes instead."

His temper flared at the accusation, but he forced himself to remain calm. "I didn't bribe anyone. What Donna had done was unfair, but I couldn't stop the hearing, so I thought I'd call as many of the selectmen as I could—"

"As many as you could? Who else did you talk to?"

"Roberts and Gilman. And I didn't offer anything or make any promises. All I did was remind them how important The Blue Creek is to this town as a thriving business and how successful it's become since you've taken over. Of course, I didn't have the financial or historical data to back me up—"

"You spoke to four selectmen?"

"And not very successfully. Roberts and Gilman voted against you anyway and Daniel sounded doubtful when we talked, but I guess you changed his mind."

"That doesn't change the fact that what you did was—"

"Wrong. One hundred percent wrong. I know that now,

but you did it, you're the one who changed his mind." He gripped Racy's shoulders. "You got the votes you needed from people I couldn't reach. You convinced them keeping The Blue Creek as is, running in your capable hands, was the right thing to do."

Her fists dropped to her sides, her shoulders sagged and the fight left her. "I can't believe you did that."

"I wasn't trying to hurt you. I wanted to fix things."

"Gage, you aren't responsible for this town and everyone in it. You can't fix everything." Racy sighed and shrugged from his touch. "This wasn't your problem to fix anyway."

He hated to do it, but he stepped back. "You're right. It was yours, and you did it beautifully. I should've had faith you'd reach the selectmen and the members of the betterment committee, even if they all didn't vote in your favor."

She closed her eyes and turned away. Silence stretched between them. "Okay, I was wrong about what you tried to do for me and you were wrong to think I needed your help. Let's leave it at that." She turned back and tapped the paperwork. "There is one thing we both can fix."

There was no way he was picking up that pen. "You know what? I think you ran away to Laramie because you got scared."

She spun back to him. "What?"

"You are so used to being alone that the idea of a date— with me or anyone else—is something you can't handle."

"You're out of your mind."

"Husband number one died because his love for the bottle was stronger than his love for you. Husband number two up and walked away and you've been alone ever since." The words poured out of his mouth and he was powerless to stop them. "You flirt with every guy out there, whether he's eighteen or eighty, but you haven't been involved with anyone since Tommy left."

"And what about you? Mr. Save-The-Town-And-Everyone-In-It. I can count the number of girlfriends you've had since you came home from Virginia on one hand and still have plenty of fingers left over. Being Destiny's lone superhero is tough work, but what the hell are you waiting for?"

You.

The word exploded in his head and he clamped his jaw shut to keep it from escaping. But it was the truth. All these years and he'd been waiting for—what? The right moment? The perfect moment? Is that what Vegas had been?

"I'm sorry, Gage. That wasn't fair. What or who you've been waiting for is none of my business." Her voice was soft as she rubbed her forehead, brows drawn tight. "It's been a crazy few weeks with the wedding, finals, the betterment committee, my brothers, finding out about us—look, just sign. I'll get it back to the lawyers and we can go back to being…friends."

Friends? Did he want to be friends with Racy?

Yeah, he did. That and so much more.

And it was time for a little less talk and a lot more action.

Chapter Eleven

Gage spun her around so fast, Racy didn't have time to react.

She could only feel. Feel his arms clamped around her as he pulled her hard to his chest. Feel his mouth, coaxing hers open, and the warm, wet heat of his tongue seeking, then finding hers. Feel his hands trailing down her back until they slid beneath her pajama top to grip her hips and press her flush against him.

The shock faded and something carnal and wild took its place. She had to admit, in the middle of the madness of her out-of-control life, she'd dreamed of this moment so many times over the last two weeks.

Now it was here.

She was back in Gage's arms and he was devouring her with kisses. Kisses she returned, loving the dark, whiskey-flavored taste of him. Kisses different from what they'd shared in the early-morning hours in his living room. This time, his mouth had a frantic need, an unrestrained passion that reminded her of the first time he'd kissed her in Vegas.

Desperate to touch him, she was limited as to how far she could reach thanks to his hold on her. The smooth material of his dress pants danced under her fingertips and she stretched her hands, cupping the tightness of his backside.

A groan rumbled in his chest at her touch, making her bold. She mimicked his action by pulling him against her and rose on tiptoes, rotating her hips against the hard ridge pressed against her. Her hands moved higher and met bare skin.

It wasn't enough.

He'd freed her mouth, his lips moving to her neck. Her head fell to the side, the not-so-gentle nips on her skin just below her ear causing a moan to rush past her lips.

She fisted his shirt and tugged. "Gage, let me go."

"No, never."

A thrill at his possessive tone shot through her, and she smiled, dropping her head to the damp cotton material covering one shoulder.

"Yes." She punctuated her request with a not-so-gentle bite.

"Hey!" He straightened, his arms going lax around her. "Why'd you do that?"

"So I can do this," she whispered, sliding her hands over the defined muscles of his chest, parting his tuxedo shirt even farther. Her nails, a demure manicure in deference to the wedding, stood out against the dark hue of his skin. She looked up when his hands gripped her waist again. His eyes had turned a dark blue, almost black in color. A flash of fear crossed his features. He thought she was going to push him away.

She should.

Her practical angel, complete with flowing white robe and halo, sat at one shoulder and lectured on how history repeating itself wasn't a good thing. But a little devil, dressed in red lace and Prada high heels, urged her to listen to her heart, and all the other throbbing body parts, and enjoy herself.

Racy decided.

Her angel disappeared in a huff. The devil left with a satisfied smirk.

When her hands reached the top of his shoulders, she pushed his shirt down his arms, forcing him to release her a second time so it could fall to the floor. The relief in his eyes blazed to something hot and passionate.

She then leaned forward to trace the outline of his collar bone with her lips, balancing herself by holding tight to his defined biceps. One strong hand came up and fisted in her hair, holding her in place as his signature scent of the great outdoors, mixed with the heat of his skin, filled her.

The faint tang of expensive champagne stayed on her lips as they caressed their way up his neck until, tender and sensitive from the day's stubble on his chin, they hovered at his mouth. "Hmm, bare skin…much better."

"My thoughts exactly," he rasped.

She wasn't prepared when he spun her again and walked her backward toward the four-poster bed. The desk, now behind Gage, came into view and the divorce paperwork lying there stood out like a bright neon sign. She closed her eyes and bumped into the corner post, her head protected from the solid wood by his hand still tangled in her curls.

His mouth captured hers again and he cradled her face. His fingers moved against her scalp as he continued to kiss her senseless. Small pulls on her hair made her realize he was searching for, and removing, the numerous bobby pins of her wedding hairdo. She raised her hands and quickly removed four, letting them fall from her hands.

He pulled back from her mouth and whispered, "Let me."

The full press of his body had her again on tiptoes, fitting him perfectly against her. The flannel material of her pajamas rubbed her breasts and belly, causing her nipples to harden and her stance to widen as she welcomed him between her legs. She reached for the post behind her for balance, then dropped her hands to his arms.

"No, I like this better." He stopped his ministries to her hair, grabbed her wrists and placed her arms back over her head.

"Gage…"

She started to lower them, but he again put her hands on the post, gently curving her fingers, making it clear he wanted her to hold on.

He looked down at her, a grin raising one corner of his mouth. "Don't make me get my handcuffs, lady."

"Are they fur-lined?" Racy peeked at him through the curly lengths of hair that partly covered one side of her face, unable to stop her own smile. "Mine are red and fuzzy. You know, to protect the delicate skin of one's wrists in case—"

"When and where," he cut her off, "did you last have a reason to use those?"

Never, but she wasn't going to tell him that. "A lady doesn't speak of such things."

One finger gently moved the curls, tucking them behind one ear. "When did you last do this? Make love to someone?"

She swallowed hard. His assertions earlier that she was too scared to be involved with anyone—especially him— had hit a little close to home. But she wasn't going to lie. She couldn't.

"Last summer. With you."

"And before that?"

He'd asked her the same question in their Vegas hotel room, moments before he'd joined his body with hers, surrounded by bubbles in that oversize tub. When she'd told him it had been over a year, he'd slowed, allowing her body to get used to him. He'd been so deliberate and gentle, she'd sworn she was going to explode from the need to have him deep inside her.

"You know the answer. You asked me in—"

"Vegas." He finished the sentence with her, his eyes bright. "You remember that?"

She nodded, tightening her hold to the post. "I remember."

His mouth came crashing down again and it took all her strength not to let go. Her body arched, pushing her fabric-covered breasts against his chest. Then she felt his fingers making quick work of the buttons. He parted the top and broke free from her mouth, his gaze on hers as he covered, then cupped her breasts with his hands. She jumped at his touch.

"Cold hands?"

Racy nodded. Then his thumbs rasped over her nipples, and she was powerless to keep her eyes open. A low mew escaped, despite biting down on her bottom lip. Wet heat from his mouth engulfed her as he pulled first one nipple, then the other, between his lips.

He knelt before her, his mouth and hands concentrating on her breasts, stomach and hips. His lips slid over her belly button, his tongue playing with the tiny martini-glass-shaped charm that hung there.

"This is so sexy." His voice rumbled against her skin. Her stomach muscles clenched, causing the drawstring waistband to slip even farther down her hips. "When'd you get it?"

"Ah, the weekend after Vegas."

He paused, his fingers tightening on her hips. "Why?"

Racy's breath hitched. "Huh?"

"Why did you get it?"

"I've wanted one for a long time."

He pulled back. She knew he was looking up at her. A

dip of her head told her she was right when her gaze collided with his.

"Why?" he repeated.

"I needed a distraction," she finally admitted, knowing his pit-bull determination wasn't going to let this go. "From the memories."

His mouth curved into a smile that could've been labeled mocking if it weren't for the naked joy in his eyes. His mouth was back on her skin and then moved lower. She felt her pants slip silently to the floor. Her overhead grip on the bedpost tightened even more, her fingers sliding down behind her head as Gage slowly dragged her lacy white thong down her hips, the fabric scraping every inch of her skin on its way to her toes.

His hands wrapped around her thighs, coaxing and caressing. Combined with the gentle pressure of his mouth, it left her powerless as her hips rocked in silent invitation. Deep in her center coiled a hunger that could only be sated with his touch, his kiss. His mouth moved closer, his beard leaving a trail of fiery heat on her skin until he finally reached her core.

Pleasure ripped though her as he loved her with his tongue, his mouth, his hands. She cried out when her release came too soon. Unable to keep her hands in place any longer, they fell to his shoulders, fingertips biting into his skin as he drove her higher and higher in an arching spiral of heated euphoria. She shivered as ripples of sexual energy echoed through her veins.

Gage finally rose and pulled her into the welcoming heat of his arms. "Still cold, baby?"

She shook her head, unable to find her voice as another shudder racked her body.

"Why don't you get under the covers, anyway?"

Racy had no idea where she got the strength, but she

crawled across the plush quilts to snuggle beneath, the cool sheets welcome against her heated skin. Numerous pillows cradled her head and despite the heaviness of her eyelids, she opened them when she didn't feel the weight of Gage following her.

Damn, look at her.

A wanton angel, naked except for the satisfied smile on her face—a smile he'd put there—surrounded by mounds of blankets. Her red curls spread over the pillows and spilled down her bare shoulders. She'd pulled the top blanket to her breasts, the lace edging not quite covering them.

Gage stood beside the bed, his hands already at the fastener on his pants, ready to strip down and join her. He was hard, painfully so, every muscle tense and throbbing and wanting nothing more than to finish what they'd started.

And then do it again. And again.

But he couldn't move. The sight of her crawling over the bedcovers on her hands and knees had poleaxed him to the spot. When she'd finally crawled beneath the covers, he'd almost felt as if he was being shut out, not welcomed in the bed, in her body.

He wanted her. He wanted her with a ferociousness he'd never felt before in his life, but he had to know that she wanted him the same way. She had to invite him.

So he waited.

"Gage?"

Every muscle in his body tightened even more. "Yeah?"

She propped herself on one arm and lifted the blankets, revealing the lush nakedness of breasts and curves and legs. "Aren't you going to join me?"

At her words, he toed off his shoes as his fingers fumbled with the zipper. He left his pants hanging loose at his waist as he bent and yanked off his socks. He rose again, slid his wallet from his back pocket, then grabbed at the waistband of both his pants and boxers when he heard a feminine snicker.

"What is that—are those cartoon boxers on your... boxers?"

Gage looked away from the grin on Racy's face to glance at the caricatures of muscle-bound fighters, complete with red boxing gloves, patterned on his underwear and he grinned. "Yeah, they were a gift from the bride."

She stretched across the bed, leaning in to get a closer look. "From Maggie?"

He let his pants fall to his ankles and stepped out of them. He dropped his wallet to the bedside table and braced his hands on his hips, knowing the cotton fabric of the boxers did little to hide his arousal.

"They're cute." She inched forward on her elbows and he felt her breath on his skin. "Did all the guys in the wedding party get a pair?"

"Yeah, I think so." His words came out a harsh whisper as she traced the waistline of the boxers with one finger.

"All the same design?"

His muscles jumped when her lips pressed against his stomach. He watched her mouth slowly follow the waistband, from the center to one hip, leaving behind a trail of wet kisses.

"Gage?"

"W-what?" He struggled to remember what the hell she had asked him. Boxers...wedding party...same design. "No I think Chase's had the Texas state flag and Bryce's had dollar bills—"

The air vanished from his lungs, robbing him of his breath and the ability to speak as she hooked a couple of fingers into the waistband and tugged downward, her mouth following.

The control he'd fought for since entering this room, hell, since Vegas, slowly gave way as she stroked and skimmed the hard length of him. It crumbled when she slid her thumb over the tip and threatened to shatter completely when the moist heat of her mouth covered him.

Gage fisted his hands in her hair, silently commanding her to stop. She ignored him and pushed him closer to the edge. With a feral growl, he stepped away from her, ridding himself of the boxers before following Racy back beneath the covers.

She tried to pull him on top of her, but he braced himself to sweep one hand down the length of her. "Racy, are you—"

She pressed her hand to his mouth, cutting off his words. "Don't ask if I'm sure. If I didn't want to be here, if I didn't want you here with me, *like this*, I would've made that one hundred percent clear…long before now."

One long leg curved over his hip as her hands did the same around his neck. She arched her back, her breasts brushing against his chest, her breath hot in his ear. "I'm not drunk. I'm not looking for revenge. What's happening between us, here and now, is all that matters. I'm not expecting anything else."

Was he expecting something? Was this supposed to be a beginning for them? A way to show her how he felt, how good they could be together?

"Love me, Gage. Just love me."

He did. He did love her. With a sudden clarity of vision, a sureness of purpose, he knew this woman—his wife—was the only woman he'd ever wanted.

He pulled away long enough to get a condom from his wallet and sheath himself. Then he was back in her arms. He rolled her beneath him and covered her with his body, filling her with his power, his need, his want…for her.

"Racy, I do lov—"

Her mouth all but consumed his in a searing, demanding kiss. Her hips rose to meet him, her legs wrapped around him, urging him deeper and harder. He complied and she took all he gave, clinging to him, matching his demanding thrusts, again and again, until she had given all of herself, and he matched her cry of surrender with his own.

For a long time he lay there, until he was able to breathe again. Then he separated their bodies and stretched out next to her. She shifted into his arms with a deep sigh, her head resting over his heart, her breathing slow and steady. She was asleep. He grinned, humbled at how natural it felt to hold her like this, and tightened his arms around her.

She wasn't ready to hear his words of love. Her kiss cutting off his declaration told him that much, but he'd get the chance to say it again. He was sure of it.

Feeling his eyelids grow heavy, he forced himself to get out of bed and clean up. He then went to turn off the only light, a small lamp on the desk. His eyes strayed to the paperwork lying there. Two sets that looked alike except for the top lines of text in bold black print.

Buyout Proposal, and Petition for Divorce.

He looked over his shoulder to the bed. His breath caught as he found Racy turned on her side, the blankets pulled aside to reveal the smooth length of her back and that sexy backside, still sound asleep.

He concentrated on the paperwork again. He'd been shocked to find out she wanted to own The Blue Creek. Max had often complained the Wyoming winters were getting harder to deal with, but Gage'd never heard him mention retiring or selling the bar. He had no idea what kind of money was involved, but from what he'd already read, Racy was planning to use her entire savings, including her Vegas winnings, as a down payment.

Was it enough? Would she be able to qualify for a loan to cover the rest? Max thought of Racy as a daughter. Maybe he'd give her a break. Still, it took money to start over again, especially if Max planned to head someplace warmer.

Maybe he should talk to him. Max always said he owed the Steeles a favor after Gage's father had saved his life when thieves had tried to rob the bar years ago. Gage had planned to call in the marker when it came to Gina's employment, but Racy had shown up before he'd been able to play the "good turn" card, but now—

Stop.

Gage shook his head. Jeez, didn't he ever learn? Look what had happened the last time he'd tried to help her. His fingers moved to the divorce papers, softly drumming as he glanced at the fireplace, nothing now but fiery embers. It would be so easy. A few seconds and they'd be nothing but smoke and ash. The temptation crawled inside his gut, but he knew getting rid of the physical evidence wouldn't change a thing.

A shiver raced through him. He blamed it on the chilly night air and quickly banked the fire, checked the door and positioned his cell phone on the bedside table before returning to Racy's side. He slid in to spoon against her, his front to her back, skin to skin.

She murmured something low he couldn't hear as she laced her fingers through his and continued to sleep. He left a small kiss on her ear before whispering, "Good night, Mrs. Steele."

Chapter Twelve

Gage awoke the next morning to bright shafts of sunlight streaming through lace curtains and the hiss and clang of the antique radiator. Alone. He reached out to the empty spot next to him. Faint heat from Racy's body clung to the bedding. The toilet flushed, then running water sounded.

Relief washed over him. He relaxed into the pillows and pulled the blankets up to his chest. He propped his hands behind his head, surprised she'd awakened before him. She'd been exhausted. It'd been a rough month for her and he hadn't helped, even when he'd tried to. But last night had been the start of something new, something better, for the both of them.

So what if they hadn't followed the traditional way to getting married? Hell, they hadn't even been on an official date. That was something he planned to change right away. They belonged together. He liked the sound of that. Together.

The water turned off and Gage closed his eyes. He'd

wait until Racy crawled back into bed before letting her know just how awake he was. Without the benefit of sight, his other senses went on full alert. He heard the creak of the bathroom door opening. A minty scent meant she'd brushed her teeth. He slowed his breathing and remained still, but the blankets didn't stir. Her weight never shifted the mattress.

He heard light footsteps as she moved around the room. A rustling noise near the fire instantly reminded him he'd seen an overnight bag near the chairs. He opened one eye a tiny crack.

She was leaving. Already dressed in jeans and a gray sweat jacket, she had her boots in one hand, her purse in the other.

Oh, hell no.

He looked at the desk—the folder of paperwork was gone, but her keys still lay there. She must have spotted them, too. He waited until she had them in her grasp before he shot out of the bed, wrapped her in his arms and yanked her backward.

"Oh!"

They tumbled back onto the bed, her boots and purse flying from her hands. He easily held her down with one leg over hers, scooting out of the way when she tried to take advantage of his nakedness with a well-placed knee or hip.

Grabbing her wrists, he trapped them on the bed and leaned over her. "Going somewhere?"

Racy squirmed and bucked, but it was like trying to move a brick wall. A very muscular, very sexy brick wall that didn't budge an inch. It reminded her of the amazing way this man had made love to her last night.

Right after he'd almost spilled the dreaded *L* word.

"I asked you a question."

His words, more like a low growl, set off the familiar

internal sparklers that would soon turn into incredible, mind-blowing, resistance-crumbling fireworks.

She gave up the fight and glared at him. "Get off me."

"No." His blue eyes darkened.

Desire mixed with a hint of anger shined in their depths and her breath disappeared. "You weigh a ton. I can't breathe."

It was true, sort of. But her inability to inhale had more to do with the hard arousal pressed against her thigh than his actual weight.

He shifted his upper body to the left, but dropped his head closer, his mouth inches away from hers. "Better?"

No, his powerful lower half still had her pinned. "You know it's not."

"You're right. Now, spill."

She turned away and stared at the wall. "Spill what—ah…" The brush of his lips on her neck had her biting back a moan. "Wh-what are you doing?"

"Being persuasive," he whispered before kissing her again. This time his lips moved from her ear to her collarbone and back again. "Hmm, you smell good."

It took all her strength not to respond with the same sentiment. He smelled as good as he had last night when she'd fallen asleep on him. Literally. When she'd woken this morning, she'd had to admit it was the best night's sleep she'd had in months.

And despite her pledge to not get emotionally involved, she'd screwed up again.

Being in the moment, throwing their cares to the wind, doing it one more time for old times' sake, should've been enough. It was what she'd been going for when she'd blocked out the sight of the divorce papers and listened to her body.

And her heart.

It was why she'd made that pretty little speech about not

expecting anything from him. Of course, practically begging him to love her probably hadn't helped. So when he'd tried to speak, she'd stopped him with a fervent kiss. She couldn't stand the idea that something he might say in the heat of passion would turn into something he'd regret in the light of day.

But then he'd wrapped her in his arms, kissed her good-night and called her Mrs. Steele. And she was right on the edge of falling for the fairy tale, complete with the prince on a white horse and the happily-ever-after. She was hanging on to reality with the tips of her fingers, and that scared the crap out of her, which was why she'd decided to do what she did best.

Run.

"Gage, please…"

He must have picked up on the desperation in her voice, because he backed off and released her wrists. She tried to push against one beefy shoulder, but the feel of his fingers on her cheek froze her in place.

He applied gentle pressure until she was forced to turn back to him. "What's going on, Racy? Talk to me."

Oh, damn, she didn't know how to deal with this kind of Gage Steele. Sweet and sexy and very appealing. When he was being a pain in the ass, yeah, he was still appealing, but she could give back as good as she got. This…this Gage she had no defenses against.

"Noth-nothing. I just need to…ah, to get home and clean up my place." She latched on to the best—okay, the first—reason that popped into her head. At least it was the truth.

He propped up on an elbow, still keeping her immobile. "You're sneaking out because you need to clean?"

"Yes, I had my place bombed yesterday."

One eyebrow arched. *Here we go again.* "Excuse me?"

"An exterminator came in and fumigated. I know… January and bugs don't mix, but they do for me. Anyway, I figured I'd be gone all day with the wedding and after the reception I'd find a place to crash—"

"So any bed last night would've worked for you?"

A direct hit and they were back in familiar territory. "*You're* the one who followed me up here!"

"All I'm asking for is a little honesty."

She pulled a deep breath. Big mistake.

Her breasts rubbed against him. His jaw clenched and his hand slid to the back of her neck, his fingers starting a rhythmic massage. He looked like he was going to kiss her again, on the mouth this time.

"Look, having spent most of the last week pissed off over a misunderstanding totally drained me." The words tumbled from her. "But I was confused and mad and trying to deal with my finals while staying upbeat for Maggie."

"You told me that last night. Before we made love."

She sighed. "Gage, last night was…was…"

"Amazing? Mind-blowing? Awesome?"

"Inevitable."

That stopped him.

"You and I have had this…thing between us for a long time," she continued, taking advantage of his stunned silence. His words describing last night branded her heart. "What happened in Vegas was just the coming together of—of—I don't know, the right cosmic forces or the alignment of the planets with both of us in the same place, same time—"

"So what does that make last night? A final itch you had to scratch?"

Racy paused, unsure how to answer.

Over the last five months, she'd spent the same amount of time mad at him, for one thing or another, as she had fantasizing about the passionate night they'd shared in Vegas. She'd wondered, even after that kiss in his living room, if being together could've possibly been *that* good.

It had.

So, they had good—no, make that *great* sex, in common, but little else.

He wasn't like any of the other men she'd had in her life. He embodied everything good and decent and true. He was strong and loyal and committed to his family and this town. He took care of everyone—even her—despite the craziness it brought to his life. She could never live up to that standard, no matter how hard she tried.

"Racy, this is going to seem like a crazy question…"

His voice yanked her out of her musings. She tried to swallow the lump in her throat, but every muscle in her body froze and refused to cooperate.

Ohmigod—he wasn't going to—even though technically they already—no, he couldn't actually be—

"Is this my sweat jacket?" he asked.

She blinked, then watched his gaze travel over the tattered, well-washed gray zippered jacket she'd thrown on this morning in her haste to get dressed.

"Huh?"

"I asked if this—" He reached for the jacket collar.

Racy knew he was looking for the white hand-stitched tag with his initials. The tag was now yellow and faded with age. The G and M were gone, as was most of the S, but the faint outline was still there.

"I'll be damned, it is! Where'd you get—" Realization dawned in his eyes. "Just before graduation…that afternoon in my truck out at the lake. You kept it? All this time?"

She shrugged and aimed for nonchalant. "Yeah, well, it's been in the back of my closet for years."

He fingered the well-worn cuff on one sleeve, then the

repaired bottom edge. His fingers skimmed across her belly, his touch hot on her already heated skin. Her muscles clenched as he traced the zipper upward until he reached where the metal pull rested between her breasts.

"You're lying. You've worn this before. You've worn it often. In fact—" he lowered his head until their noses touched, his words a hot rush over her lips "—you had it on the day I told you we were still marr—"

The shrill ring of his cell phone cut off his words.

Gage squeezed his eyes shut and gutted out a couple of coarse, but softly spoken, curse words.

Racy waited until he sat up and put the phone to his ear to wiggle away from him, trying not to look at the magnificent naked body on display.

"Steele here."

She reached for her boots and tugged them on, knowing he watched her every move.

"What? When? Has the fire department been called?" He sat up straight, and shoved a hand through his dark hair as every muscle in his abdomen flexed. "How bad is it?"

His clipped tone caused her to pause, but she had to get out of there while she could. Her purse had landed under the desk. Where the hell had her keys gone?

The blue-and-white logo of The Blue Creek key ring nestled in the jumbled bedding caught her eye. Success.

"What's the location? Is it commercial or…ah, dammit!"

His hand clamped down on hers as she grabbed her keys. "Hey!"

"I'm on my way." He said into his phone then ended the call. "Racy, wait."

"I can't." She twisted her wrist, surprised when he let go. "I need to get going and it sounds like you have some pressing—"

He scooted to the edge of the bed. "Where's Jack?"

"What?" She backed up a step. "Why would you ask—"

He grabbed his underwear from the floor and slipped them on. "Racy, answer me. Where's Jack?"

"Out at Maggie's ranch. I told you my place was being fumigated. Do you really think I'd leave—ohmigod…you said fire department. Is it…is it my house?"

He started toward her, six-plus feet of solid muscle, looking ridiculously sexy in nothing but those red, white and blue cartoon boxers. Compassion and pity filled his dark eyes. "It's gonna be okay—"

"Ohmigod, it is." An unfathomable horror filled her. No! Not her house, not now! "My house is on fire."

"Let me get dressed—" Gage reached for his tuxedo pants. "Dammit, we need to stop by my office. I've got clothes there."

"No." She backpedaled from his outstretched hand, stumbling over her duffel bag. "I need to go. I need to go now."

"Racy—"

She grabbed her bag, the webbed handles pressing into her palm as a sick thought filled her head. Its contents might be all she had left in the world. "I have to go home."

She rushed from the room and flew down the stairs. Jumping into her Mustang, she gunned it to life. Snow and slush spraying from her tires, she raced out of the parking lot. Mindful of the Saturday-morning crowds, she blessed every traffic light that went her way as she headed down Destiny's main street.

The sight of kids playing in the snow with their dogs had her sending a quick prayer of thanks her precious pet wasn't at home. The tears she refused to allow to fall stung the back of her eyes, blurring her vision. She brushed them away and opened the driver's-side window, welcoming the rush of cold air on her face. Once on the outskirts of town, she picked up speed.

She knew better.

She knew better than to dream, to plan, to believe. It always came back to bite her in the ass.

But not this time, please, not this time.

Ten minutes later she turned onto her road and the smell of smoke rushed in her open window. Ohmigod, it was real. It really was happening.

Her fingers clenched the wheel as she slowed for the last bend, bright orange-and-yellow flames visible through the trees. A half-dozen pickup trucks crowded the long drive, forcing her to park on the side of the road. Her car slid into a snowbank when she hit the brakes and she scrambled out, leaving the door open behind her.

A stomach-turning, nose-burning stench hit her full in the face as she sped up her snow-and-dirt driveway. Someone called her name, but she didn't stop. She staggered around the end of one of the fire department pickup trucks and was blasted with a flash of red-hot heat.

Mesmerized, she stared at her home, completely engulfed in flames that shot out of every window and through the roof.

It was gone. All gone.

"Racy! What are you doing? Get back!"

A pair of hands gripped her and yanked her backward. She tried to pull away, but the fingers wouldn't let go.

"Don't fight me, girl. You need to get away from here."

She spun around and found Leeann tugging on her arm. "Lee, what are you—what happened? What's going on?"

"Come on, hon, let the firefighters do their jobs." Her friend wrapped an arm around her, forcing Racy to move back behind the main fire truck.

Numbness took over as she watched Destiny's volunteer firefighters, including Devlin Murphy, who barked out orders from the side yard. Many were regulars at The Blue Creek and she'd always joked she expected great service if she ever needed to call on them.

"It's gone," she whispered. "It's all gone. I tried…tried to do it right…but I screwed up. Again. Am I ever going to learn?"

Leeann grabbed a blanket and wrapped it around her shoulders. "You must be freezing. And don't panic yet. They might be able to save—"

"Save what?" she cried. "Look at it! Everything I have…my life…is in that house."

"Jack is safe, right? You told me at the reception he was at Maggie's."

"Y-yes, he is, thank God, but you don't understand—"

"I do understand." Leeann set the blanket back over Racy's shoulders. "Better than most."

Of course she did. "Oh, Lee, I'm sorry. I didn't think about your family's home being destroyed by fire."

"That was years ago and no one was living there at the time, so it's not the same, but I do know what you're going through." Leeann pulled her into a hug. "Now, is there a chance anyone else was inside your place?"

Racy shook her head.

Leeann backed up, but kept her hands on Racy's arms. "Billy Joe or Justin?"

Her heart lurched. She again shook her head, then thought about the exterminator's visit. She told Leeann, who grabbed a passing firefighter and relayed the information.

"You don't think—"

Leeann shook her head, cutting her off. "No, you said the appointment was yesterday morning. I just wanted Murphy to know because of the chemicals involved."

"Do you think that's the reason?"

"I don't know, honey."

"How did…how did you know about this?"

"I was at the station about to get in my cruiser when Gage came zooming into the parking lot. He told me about the fire as he headed inside. To change I guess." Leeann bit down on her bottom lip. "He was still dressed in his tux from last night."

Racy's anger burned as hot as the fire. "What else did he tell you?"

"What?"

"Did he tell you about our fight? How badly I screwed up? But that I was actually trying to entice him up to my room?" She knew she was being unreasonable, but with everything happening she wasn't thinking straight. "Did he tell you how drunk I—?"

"Hey, you only had a few glasses of champagne."

"Not that kind of drunk. No, that's an easy drunk." Her voice shook as she paced in the already trampled snow. "No, I'm talking about being drunk on living in the moment, believing in the slightest chance of happily-ever-after."

Her hands balled into fists as her emotions turned raw. "About buying into the notion that good things are possible and that a person can climb out of the box life shoved them into—"

"Racy, you're not making any sense."

"No, she isn't."

She jumped at the sound of Gage's voice. Closing her eyes, she drew a deep breath through her nose, determined not to gag on the smoke. When she opened them and turned, he stood there, dressed in his usual garb of jeans, leather bomber jacket and off-white Stetson.

"Leeann, could you give us a moment, please?" he asked.

Her friend turned away from her boss. "You okay with that?"

Racy gave a quick jerk of her head.

"I'll see if Murphy has anything to report." She looked back at Gage, then left after he nodded in agreement.

"Let's get a bit farther from the fire, okay?"

Racy skirted away from his hand, refusing to be lulled by his soothing tone. Marching past a couple of trucks and Gage's Jeep, she finally stopped when they were near her car. "What?"

He glanced at the fire. "I know it looks bad—"

"Looks bad?" She thrust out her arm and pointed at the engulfed remains of her house. "It's gone! That was my way out. That was the collateral for my loan to buy The Blue Creek. You saw the paperwork! I want the Creek, I want it to be mine, but that's not going to happen now."

"Why?"

"Respect! I want respect. I want people in this town to look me in the eye when I walk down the street. I want people like Donna Pearson to know they can't come into *my* business and tell me how to run it."

She jabbed her chest with her thumb. "I wanted to prove it didn't matter who my father was, or how many times I was stupid enough to get married—or where I live—" She choked on her words. "Where I lived."

He moved closer, but she scurried back a few steps. She had to. She knew how to get through this. Alone.

"Racy, please, I can fix this. We can fix—"

She shook her head. "No, we can't."

"Tell me what I can do for you. I'll do anything."

"Anything?"

He put his hand over his heart. "You have my word."

It took only a minute for her to reach for the duffel bag in the front seat of her car. She came back and slapped a folded stack of papers to his chest.

"Sign this." Her voice was cold and lifeless. "Sign it and drop it off at the bar. I'll get it back to the lawyers."

Chapter Thirteen

An aging furnace had destroyed Racy's dream. Gage sat at his desk and looked again at the county fire investigator's initial report that arrived two days after the fire was extinguished.

He'd taken it home and read it over day-old pizza and a beer. Details were still needed, but the area of origin for the fire was the twenty-year-old furnace in her basement.

And she didn't have homeowner's insurance.

He'd read that in the report, too. The house was paid off years ago, so it wasn't a requirement. Racy had told the investigator she'd let the insurance lapse in order to help pay for her college education. Her plans to use the property as a loan guarantee required insurance, and she had been days away from getting it reestablished.

He'd thought about calling her as soon as he'd read the report—hell, he'd thought about calling every moment since he'd watched her red Mustang head down the road, Leeann driving and Racy curled up in the passenger seat.

He knew she and Jack were staying with Leeann. She hadn't been at The Blue Creek, much less in town, since Saturday morning, and despite what she'd said, both at the inn and at the fire, he still loved her.

What was he going to do about it? He hadn't figured it out yet. But he'd signed the divorce papers and dropped them at the bar like she'd asked. He'd hated the sound of the pen as he'd scrawled his name across the last page, but for whatever reason, at this moment, this was what Racy needed from him.

And he'd promised.

But if she thought he would just walk away…

That wasn't going to happen. He couldn't do that any more than he could refuse to take his next breath.

"Hey, you got a minute?"

Startled, he looked up. His brother Garrett stood in the doorway. Gage checked the wall clock over the teen's head. "What are you doing here? It's just after noon."

"We had a half day at school." He switched his backpack from one shoulder to the other. His football letterman jacket hung open and a Duke University T-shirt peeked out.

"Can we talk?"

It was the first time his brother had approached him since the drag racing and bonfire incidents. The only other time they'd spoken in the last couple of weeks had consisted of Gage lecturing and Garrett protesting his innocence. Gage missed the lively debates they used to have over sports, or Garrett's devotion to hip-hop versus Gage's preference for classic rock and country music.

"Sure. Take a seat." He waved at the chair in front of his desk.

Garrett stepped inside, dropped his backpack to the floor and motioned to the door. "Ah, can I close this?"

Gage's internal radar went on full alert. Was his little brother here to confess more mischievous deeds before he heard about them through official channels? "Is it necessary?"

His brother jerked his head in a quick nod.

"Okay, go ahead."

Garrett shut the door and then slouched in the wooden chair on the other side of the desk. He seemed more interested in playing with his class ring than talking, so Gage waited.

"That sucks about what happened to Ms. Dillon's house," he finally said, looking up. "Gina says she's a real nice lady."

Gage hoped his surprise at his brother's words didn't show on his face. This was the last thing he'd expected Garrett to bring up. "Ah, yeah, it does…suck."

"She's at all the home games, ya know, helping with the refreshments 'cause The Blue Creek donates food and stuff," Garrett added. "She's really pretty, too—Racy…ah, Ms. Dillon, I mean. Some of the guys on the team think she's a total hottie. You know, in a cougar sort of way—"

"Garrett, is there a point to this?" The last thing he wanted to hear was the fantasies a bunch of high school boys had about his wife.

Correction. His soon-to-be ex-wife.

"Ah, yeah. Anyway, I heard you and mom talking about what caused the fire this morning when you stopped by for breakfast. It's being ruled an accident, right?"

"That's not public knowledge yet, but it looks that way."

Not that he was a hundred percent convinced, despite what the report said.

"I didn't know if I should say anything." Garrett paused and let out a sigh. "It's probably gonna get my home confinement extended, but I thought—well, it might mean something."

He was talking in riddles. "What might?"

The kid squared his shoulders and pulled in a deep breath before releasing it with a rush of words. "On Saturday morning I snuck out and took Leenie Harden on a sunrise snowmobile ride."

Eileen Harden, the oldest of the mayor's three teenage daughters. *Wonderful.*

"How?"

"Huh?"

"I'm not even going to touch the fact that you're grounded, but where'd you get a snowmobile? Mine is locked up and the two at the house still aren't fixed."

"Oh, ah…we took her dad's."

Gage closed his eyes and tried to rub away the beginnings of a headache. "You stole it?"

"No! We borrowed it. Technically."

He dropped his hand to the desk and opened his eyes. "Technically?"

"Leenie had the key to their shed."

"Garrett, if you didn't have permission, that's steal—"

"Save the lecture until I'm done, okay? There's more."

Gage nodded and remained silent.

"So anyway, we took it out in the woods and ended up on a ridge that looks down on the highway. We stopped to wait for the sunrise. Leenie brought a blanket and some hot chocolate—"

"I really don't want to hear this."

"Give me a break, bro. We were dressed in snowsuits, boots, helmets and gloves. Do you know how hard it is to kiss a girl with a helmet on?"

"Not hard at all after you take the helmet off."

Garrett rolled his eyes. "Whatever. We were sitting there idling when the machine suddenly stopped. Leenie panicked, but I told her I could fix it. So I started poking around the engine and that's when we heard voices."

"Voices?"

"Yeah. Leenie really started to freak, so I told her I'd go see what was going on. I made my way up this small hill and at the top, I looked down and realized we were right over Racy Dillon's place."

His brother had Gage's full attention now. He and Racy had still been wrapped in each other's arms that early on Saturday morning. "What did you see?"

"Two men. They were carrying boxes up out of the basement, through the bulkhead, and loading them into a pickup truck. I think it was her brothers."

A hard knot formed in his stomach. "Why would you think that? What did the men look like?"

"Average height, but one was a bit taller and broader through the shoulders. The other looked heavier, all stomach. Both wore jeans, work boots, flannel shirts and ball caps."

Impressed, Gage wrote down his brother's descriptions. "That's very detailed."

"You always say the attention's in the details. Runs in the family, I guess."

He smiled. "Yeah, I guess so. But why do you think it was Billy Joe and Justin Dillon?"

"One of the men, the bigger one called the fatter one Billy. When the man popped his head out of the bulkhead his ball cap fell off. It was Billy Joe Dillon."

Gage's mind raced with questions. What the hell were Racy's brothers doing at her place, especially since both lived elsewhere? And what were they taking from her house at that time in the morning?

"Did you see what was in the boxes? How big were they?"

Garrett shook his head, hair falling into his eyes as he gestured with his hands. "I don't know, two feet by two feet?"

More note taking. "Did you get a look at the truck?"

"It was red I think, but it was filthy. It had a camper shell, black. I couldn't see inside."

"What about a license plate?"

"Darn, I never thought of that." Garrett ran his hand through his hair, pushing it off his face. "Sorry, bro."

"Hey, you did a good job bringing this to me." Gage looked up from the notebook. His brother's grin was so much like their dad's. "Anything else? Did they see you?"

"No, I don't think so. I was crouched behind a couple of fallen logs. They weren't really doing anything wrong, but I've heard the Dillon brothers don't have the best track record when it comes to being upstanding citizens, ya know?" He shrugged. "I guess instinct told me to stay out of sight."

"Then what?"

"Then I left. It had only been about ten minutes, but Leenie was alone. So I went back and luckily got the snowmobile going again and took her home. I was on the couch chowing on a bowl of cereal by eight o'clock."

The estimated ignition time of the fire. "Have you told anyone about this?"

He shook his head. "Like I said, I didn't really think about it until everyone was talking about the fire in school yesterday. I mean, it's their sister's house. Why would they do anything to her?"

Gage could think of numerous reasons and all of them illegal. He jammed the notebook in his shirt pocket and stood. "I want you to keep this to yourself for now. We're going to have to fill out some official paperwork on what you witnessed, but right now I need to do some checking."

He grabbed the fire report and walked around the desk as his brother rose, slinging his backpack over one shoulder. Gage reached for his jacket and Stetson, shoving the report in an inside pocket.

"Ah, Gage?"

He opened the door, then looked at his brother. "Yeah?"

"Am I in trouble for sneaking out?"

Gage paused for a moment before he answered. "I think we'll let this one slide."

"Cool." Relief showed in Garrett's wide smile. "Thanks."

"But I think you need to have a talk with the mayor."

He didn't wait for his brother's response. The widening of Garrett's eyes and the drop of his jaw told him it was the last thing he wanted to do. But he would. Gage would make sure of it.

He stopped at the front desk and described the pickup truck to Alison, asking her to run a check on anything that matched and report back only to him. He got in his Jeep, took a moment to double-check his weapon and headed for The Blue Creek.

Justin was the easiest of the brothers to start with. Gage hadn't been crazy about him working at the bar, but Racy had seemed confident he was on the road to redemption. Both he and Billy Joe had been quiet since that first night at Racy's.

A little too quiet.

He arrived a few minutes later, parked and went inside. Less than a dozen customers filled a few tables. Good. He walked past them all, nodding hello to a few, and sat in the last booth in the farthest corner, his back to the wall.

His gaze scanned the room again, and despite it being a part of his job, he was looking for Racy. She wasn't here. He pushed away his disappointment. It was probably for the best.

A couple of waitresses worked the tables. He was glad to see his sister wasn't one of them. Jackie, an assistant manager, was behind the bar. He caught her eye and waved. She gestured to the beer taps, but he shook his head. She brought over an ice water instead.

"Afternoon, Sheriff."

"Hey, Jackie, can I get a Blue Creek Burger and fries?"

"Sure." She leaned against the table. "Anything else?"

"Is Justin working?"

Her eyebrows rose, but she only nodded.

"Let him know I'd like to speak with him, when he gets a free moment."

"Will do."

Gage looked over his notes again, then waited. Ten minutes later, a plate of food dropped on the table with a clunk. A jar of ketchup and silverware wrapped in a napkin appeared next.

Justin stood there with his arms crossed over his chest. "You wanted to see me?"

Gage had figured he'd be the one to bring out his order once Jackie had told him who was looking for him. He squeezed a generous helping of ketchup on the plate. "Join me for a minute," he finally said.

"Is that a request or an order?"

"Whatever it takes to get you to sit."

Justin sighed, dropped his arms and slid into the booth. He automatically put both hands on the table. Fingers spread wide, the ones on his right hand tapped an off-beat cadence.

"Old habits die hard, huh?"

Justin looked at his hands, then met Gage's eyes again. "Some, I guess."

Gage mentally matched the broad shoulders and muscular build inside the dark T-shirt with Garrett's description. He'd already assessed the man was taller than average, but it was close enough. Then he noticed the small cuts and bruising on the left side of his face. "What happened?"

"Nothing. It's no big deal."

He was lying. It looked like someone had clocked him hard, but Gage moved on. "You mind telling me where you were Friday night?"

"Working."

He popped a French fry into his mouth. "Until when?"

"The Creek closes at 2:00 a.m. on the weekends, you know that." Justin's voice remained steady and even. "The kitchen stops serving at midnight. By the time I finish cleaning, it's time to help clean up the main bar."

"What'd you do after that? Between two-thirty and dawn?"

"Why? What are you—is this about the fire at Racy's?" Justin sat up straighter in his seat. "What in the hell are you accusing me of?"

A second fry paused on the way to his mouth. "I'm not accusing you of anything." Gage chewed quickly, then took a sip of water. "So?"

"I was here the whole time. Played some pool and went to bed," he finally said.

"Alone?"

Justin's hands curled into fists. "Yes."

"No."

Justin's head snapped to the side. Gage's did too at the familiar voice.

Gina.

He noticed Justin looked as thunderstruck as he felt at the sight of his sister standing there, wringing her hands together. The black Blue Creek T-shirt she wore was cinched behind her back, allowing a sliver of skin to show at her waist.

Gage couldn't believe what he'd heard. "What did you say?"

She licked her lips and took a couple steps forward until she stood at the table. "I said, no, he wasn't alone."

Gage hoped his features didn't reflect his astonishment. "Would you care to explain that statement?"

"I also worked Friday night. After we cleaned up, I left, but then I realized I'd forgotten my purse and came back inside. We…ah, we ended up…playing a few games of pool—"

"That's not what he's talking about," Justin said.

Gage looked at him, but Justin's gaze was locked with his sister's.

"Look, I know you said you didn't want anyone to know about what happened…about us, but this is important." Gina's gaze went from Justin back to him. "You think Justin is somehow connected to the fire at Racy's, right? Well, he's not because I was here…with him…all night."

This time Gage couldn't hold back a groan. He'd known nothing good would come from his sister working here, but this? He watched Justin's eyes narrow. At what? The sheriff's sister admitting she'd spent the night with him?

"She's lying," Justin said.

She spun to face him, hands on her hips. "I am not!"

Silence reigned. Gage kept his gaze on his sister and asked, "So what happened?"

She relaxed her stance, sliding her hands from her hips to the tops of her thighs. From the corner of his eye, he saw Justin watching her every move. Gina must've noticed, too, because a pink stain crept across her cheeks. "Well?"

"Like I said, we were playing pool. I'm not very good so Justin showed me a few moves. Well, one thing led to another and we ended uh—upstairs in his room…you know, this really is none of your business. I'm not a little girl anymore. I can s-spend the night—" Gina paused. "You don't really want details, do you?"

No, he didn't.

And as much as he hated to admit it, he hoped whatever had happened between them was just a onetime thing. Justin Dillon was the last person Gina should get involved with.

He glanced at Justin again. "Did you do that to him?"

Confusion filled his sister's eyes for a moment. "What are you—no! You're talking about his face? No, of course not!"

"You think your sister had to fight me off?"

No, he didn't. The intimate vibes between these two were too strong and Gina's shock at his suggestion was too genuine.

Gage sighed, and put his mind back on his job. "When did you leave?"

"Around 9:00 a.m. on Saturday."

Which meant Justin couldn't have been with Billy Joe. Damn, who would've thought his sister would end up being Justin's alibi. "You sure about this?"

"The sheets on his bed are a deep forest green, he prefers English tea to coffee and there's an alligator in his bathroom," Gina shot back. "You want to go check it out?"

This time Gage looked at Justin. "An alligator?"

Justin's eyes narrowed. "It's a stuffed animal and it was a gift from the daughter of a fellow in—an old friend."

"So, are we finished?" Gina said, with a false brightness. "Need me to put it in writing? Sign with my blood? If so, we need to get moving. My shift starts…now."

"We're finished," Gage said, then waited until Gina hurried away before he turned back to Justin. "You're free to go, too."

"You never told me what this has to do with the fire at my sister's place."

"No, I didn't."

"Is Racy in danger?"

He hoped not, but he wasn't sure. "Officially, I have to say no."

Justin sat forward. "And unofficially?"

Just because he hadn't been at Racy's place Saturday morning, didn't mean Justin didn't know what his brother was up to. "It's still an open investigation."

Justin waited a moment, then he shook his head and left the booth, heading back toward the kitchen.

Gage picked at the food, but the hamburger and fries now looked less than appetizing. He'd rather deal with Billy Joe on an empty stomach anyway. He spotted Gina on the other side of the dance floor. She looked up, but not at him. Her gaze locked on Justin as he disappeared behind the swinging door.

She followed.

Gage counted to ten before he got up, dropped enough cash on the table to cover the food and headed in the same direction. He figured he could leave the back way. He pushed through the door leading to the back hall and found the two of them in a heated discussion at the other end.

When Justin took a step closer, easily towering over his sister, Gage moved forward. Suddenly, Gina spun away, horror on her face, but stopped when she saw him. He watched her struggle with the choice of which way to go, then continued to head toward him.

"Just like I expected a little girl to react. If you're worried about me going after your sister, lawman, don't be." Justin's voice carried down the hall. "Naïveté isn't a turn-on."

Gina rushed past him and disappeared behind a door marked Staff Only. Gage wanted to follow, to make sure she was okay but he knew it was the last thing she'd want.

He headed for Justin instead.

"Must be something in the water today," Justin said. "Racy just about knocked me to the floor when she ran out of here."

Gage tried to keep up as the man switched gears on him. "Racy was here? When?"

"Earlier this morning." Justin jerked a thumb over his shoulder. "I saw her on the phone when I walked by her office. She didn't seem very happy. Next thing I know she's pushing past me to get out the door. Must've been at least a half hour ago."

Instinct told Gage this wasn't good. She could be anywhere by now. He headed for the exit, then paused and looked back.

"Hey, Dillon."

Justin looked at him.

"Next time, sleep on the damn pool table. Alone."

Chapter Fourteen

After all she'd been through and now this?

She was going to kill him!

Racy's Mustang zoomed up Razor Hill Road. She negotiated the curves like a seasoned race car driver, flashing back to high school when she and Bobby Winslow had raced on this country road. Leeann, as always, with Bobby, and Maggie riding shotgun next to her. Her daddy's truck had been fast, but she rarely beat Bobby's souped-up '75 Plymouth Duster, a car he'd loved almost as much as he'd loved Leeann.

She'd left the comfortable bubble of Leeann's house this morning, having worked up the courage to go by her place—what was left of it—only to be turned away. It would be a few more days before she could start picking through the ashes.

Afterward she'd gone to The Blue Creek, and miracle of miracles, hadn't seen Gage at all. Not that she'd expected to. While it seemed as if everyone in town had stopped by Sunday to check on her and drop off food, Gage hadn't. She'd hated that she'd found herself straining to hear his low-timbred voice every time the front door had opened. When she'd stepped into her office, she'd found a sealed envelope on her desk, her name written in a bold, masculine scrawl. The divorce papers.

She'd ignored the sharp pain that had jabbed at her stomach as she'd yanked out the paperwork, going straight to the last page. He'd signed them. Unfolding the additional piece of paper that had fallen from the tattered envelope, she'd found their original marriage license from Vegas.

Damn him!

She'd rubbed her finger over the embossed stamp in the corner and stared at their names until her ringing cell phone had broken through her daze. She'd answered the call and at first thought it was a joke. Then the picture had arrived with a text message and she'd shoved the paperwork in her purse and raced out the back door.

Jack's life was in danger.

Her stomach clenched so hard it hurt to breathe. *What kind of person did something like this?*

The ringtone of The Hollies' classic "Long Cool Woman" filled the car's interior. She looked at her cell phone's display. Restricted number. "Hello?"

"Where are you?"

"On Razor Hill Road, just past the turnoff to Becker's Ridge. Where are you?"

Billy Joe's manic laugh sent chills up her spine, but she ignored it and concentrated on the directions he gave before he hung up on her. Bastard. Why was he dragging her poor puppy into this? And way out here? And how had he discovered the amount of money in her bank account?

The old mailbox and tree stump he told her to look for

came into view. She turned down a dirt road, following the deep ruts made by another vehicle.

Her cell phone went off again. "Listen, you jerk, I just made the turnoff. I'll be there in a few minutes."

"Racy?"

Ohmigod, Gage.

"Racy? Where are you?"

"What do you want? I'm busy."

"Look something's come up. I need to talk to you."

She thought back to the marriage license. "I think we've said all we need to say."

"It's important. Where are you?"

One jerk at a time. "I'm dealing with Billy Joe. I'll see you when I get back—"

"Are you at his place over Mason's Garage?"

"No, he's got me driving out here in the middle of nowhere." Grooves and snow-covered rocks jerked the wheels to the left. She fought for control as she steered with one hand. "Ah, my poor Mustang isn't built for this damn road."

"Racy, tell me where you are. Now."

She hit the speakerphone button and propped the cell phone in her coffee mug holder. Much better. "Why? What's going on—"

"A witness placed your brother at your house the morning of the fire." She heard the suppressed alarm in Gage's voice. Her foot eased off the gas. "I've seen the preliminary reports. It states your furnace was the cause, but he was seen carting boxes out of your basement."

A trigger of fear mixed with anger. That's how he knew about her money. The bastard must have read through the bank paperwork she'd left on the kitchen table. But what the hell had he taken from her home besides Jack?

"Racy, you…there?"

Damn mountaintop reception. "You're breaking up, Gage. I'm off Razor Hill Road. Heading for the Mason hunting cabin."

"Dammit, stop…turn around."

She eyed the narrow road and the thick forest surrounding her. There was no room to maneuver her car. Not that she would have even if there was. "I can't. He's got Jack."

"What?"

"Billy Joe took Jack. He wants twenty-five thousand dollars or he's—" She bit back the panic in her voice and tried to stay calm, but she couldn't stop the sharp sting of tears. "He said he's going to kill my dog if I don't give him the money." Praying he could hear her, she rattled off Billy Joe's directions. A wooden shack came into view. "Did you get that?"

"I'm on my way, but you need to get out of there. Now."

Her grip tightened on the steering wheel. She shouldn't have rushed out of the bar half-cocked and hell-bent because of her brother's idiotic, rambling call. But it was the photo he'd sent, of Jack, muzzled with a gun pressed to his head, that had her racing out to the cabin.

Panic flooded her veins. "I can't turn back. I need to get Jack."

"Racy, you should've called me."

"I can take care of this myself. I don't need your help."

Gage's sigh reached over the airwaves. "I know how much you love that dog, but please wait until I get there. We'll come up with something, a plan to save—"

"Too late." She pulled into the clearing, noting the pickup there. "Billy Joe just walked outside."

"Don't get out of the car. Lock your doors."

She hit the brakes. Her Mustang lurched to a stop. Clothes disheveled and a scraggly beard on his too-pale face, her brother looked like he hadn't slept in days. But it was what he held in his hands that took her breath. "H-he's got a gun. He's waving it at me and yelling for me to get out."

"Racy, don't—"

"I'm leaving my phone on so you can t-track me." She barely moved her lips, hoping Gage could still hear her. "I'll do what I do best and keep him talking."

"Racy—"

"Hurry, okay?"

The words rushed out of her mouth before she could stop them, exposing her fear but also her belief that he'd get here in time. She knew he would.

Blinking hard, Racy slammed the lid on the riot of emotions battling inside and opened the car door. After a deep breath, she greeted her brother like he'd expect her to. "What in the hell are you doing, Billy Joe?"

"It's about time you showed up." He staggered in the snow and used the gun to point at the cabin's doorway. "Give me your keys and get inside."

Her fingers tightened, the metal of her keys biting into her skin. Was he drunk, too? With a loaded gun?

"It's freezing up here. Let's go somewhere else and talk."

"Like your place?" Another burst of frenzied laughter. "Oh, yeah, you don't have a place anymore. Come on, toss over the keys and get your ass inside. Your precious pooch is waiting for you." This time the gun stopped waving. He aimed directly at her as his voice turned deadly. "Now."

Her heart jumped to her throat, cutting off her ability to speak. She tossed her key ring at him, then headed for the door.

Once inside, she went straight for Jack, who sat in the middle of the room leashed to a cold woodstove. Trying to wrestle his way out of the muzzle over his snout, he greeted her with a thumping tail.

Her fingers worked on the leather straps as Billy Joe

walked in and kicked the door shut. "Why are you doing this?" she asked him.

"You know why. What are you doing?"

"Jack can't breathe properly. I'm taking this damn thing off."

"Girl, you are just like a mama to that beast." Billy Joe bent over and grabbed a beer from the top of an old ice chest. It was the only thing in the room. Other than an old metal bed covered with a sleeping bag—and the many empties on the floor. "I knew that mutt would get me what I wanted. How'd you get all that money you've got stashed away? Whatcha been doing? Skimming from the bar?"

"I've been saving."

Billy Joe snorted. "Yeah, right. Don't lie to me, girlie."

Racy looked at him, but her gaze caught on the open door behind him. It had failed to catch after Billy Joe had entered, and it had bounced open again. It was their only way out. "I won big in Vegas last summer. Playing poker. Remember when Daddy taught you, me and Justin how to play?"

"Yeah, I remember. He taught us how to cheat."

"I didn't cheat. I won it fair and square." She finally got the muzzle free and yanked it from Jack's head. He rewarded her with a flurry of kisses.

"Who cares? You got a check for me?"

"Billy, I have plans for that money."

"Me, too. I'm heading for Canada and that's gonna help me set up my new operation."

"What operation?" She kept her hand on Jack's collar, ready to release him from his leash.

"God, you are dumb." He moved closer. "You never go into your basement, do ya?"

Gage's words came rushing back. "What are you talking about?"

"Damn, girl, before we even showed our faces, I was

back in that house. But I was quiet as a mouse. You never knew I was there."

He was right. With her washer and dryer in the kitchen, she had rarely gone into the basement and certainly not during the last hectic few weeks. "Why would—my God, what were you doing?"

"Let's just say I'm back in business."

Her bewilderment must have shown on her face.

"Oh, come on. I had a good little drug-run setup years ago, all the way into Canada. It didn't take long to get back in the game. Now I've got a chance to get into the big bucks, but it takes money to make money." Billy Joe grinned and motioned to her and Jack with his gun. "I knew you'd never hand it over if I asked nicely. So I decided you needed a bit more incentive."

Drugs? In her house? "Was the fire your doing?"

"Did I set it deliberately? Naw, but who cares. Now, hand over that check."

"I…I don't understand…"

He threw his beer across the room and kicked at the nearby ice chest, sending empty bottles flying toward her. "I've got people waiting. Give it to me."

Adrenaline rushed through her, changing her confusion to fear and then to anger. She wasn't going down without a fight. Gage was on his way. He'd said so. How long would it take? She needed to get out of the cabin. Without her keys, her car was useless. The woods were their best defense.

One of the empty bottles rested at her feet. She released Jack from the leash. He lurched as if wanting to run but stayed put, body quivering with suppressed energy. If she could knock out Billy Joe or at least get a head start—

"What's it going to be?" He moved closer and aimed the gun he was holding at her. "You gonna hand it over or do I have to take it from you?"

"Would you please point that thing somewhere else?" The words rasped over her dry throat.

"Ya never did like guns, did ya?" Billy Joe lifted the revolver, cradling it in both hands, bringing it upward to point at an imaginary target. "Remember those shotguns Daddy had? I used to wish he'd take me hunting—"

"Let her go, Billy Joe. Now."

Gage's command filled the air. Jack reacted and sprang at her brother, jaws clamping down on his wrist. Blasts of gunfire and her brother's scream rang in her ears. She cried out as Billy Joe crumpled to the floor, landing on top of her. She pushed until he rolled off, clutching his blood-stained leg.

Then she saw Gage lying in the open doorway.

"No!" The scream tore from her chest as she crawled on her hands and knees, reaching him as more of Destiny's finest rushed into the clearing.

"Gage!" She ignored demands to stay still and grabbed at his hand clutching his chest. Blood seeped through his fingers. "Ohmigod, he's been shot. Get help! Get help now!"

She turned his face toward her, praying she'd see his beautiful blue eyes looking back at her. Lids closed, he remained still. "Gage, stay with me. Please, stay...don't leave me—don't leave...I love you—"

She bit hard at her bottom lip, cutting off her outburst as the shock of her admission hit her.

Oh, God, she loved him.

Racy Dillon loved Gage Steele.

A blur of activity surrounded her as people swarmed over them and moved past her toward Billy Joe. Jack sat nearby and growled when a deputy reached for the gun he held in his jaw, then released it.

"Are you hurt, Ms. Dillon?" Hands grabbed at her. "Let us help—"

"I'm fine," she cried, thrashing her shoulders, struggling to free herself. "It's not me, it's Gage. Please, help him."

"We will, but you need to get back."

"No, please, I don't want to leave him."

Her plea was useless as someone pulled her away. Jack rushed to her side as her unblinking eyes settled on the man she'd finally admitted loving, looking for any sign of life.

The man she was one hundred percent certain was all wrong for her had somehow found a way past the bravado and boldness she'd used since childhood to protect herself. The boy who'd been her first crush, her first real kiss, was the man who'd shown her what physical love could be between a man and a woman. Tender, playful, passionate, daring. Giving and taking, sharing and exploring.

But he was so much more than that.

As certain as she was of her feelings, she was equally certain he deserved a woman who could be everything he needed, who would be worthy of him. She wasn't that woman.

She didn't remember getting into the ambulance with Gage but she couldn't look away from the stillness of his features, her eyes willing him to wake up. The EMTs worked frantically, speaking in medical jargon she didn't understand, as they hooked him up to an IV and placed an oxygen mask over his face.

He can't die. He can't die.

They arrived at a hospital and she realized they'd driven all the way to Laramie. Oh, God, what did that mean? Destiny's clinic couldn't handle Gage's injuries?

She was rushed into an exam room while a crowd of medical personnel disappeared down a long corridor with Gage.

He'd never woken up, never said a word.

She let them check her over and repeated all she knew about Billy Joe to the deputies. They told her Jack had been taken to the station for safekeeping and, when the nurse requested her closest family member, she gave Justin's name.

And she asked about Gage.

Again and again she asked, but no one could tell her anything. She had no idea how much time passed. Then Justin was at her side, telling her she was being released.

"I'm not going anywhere."

"Racy—"

"Forget it." She pushed him out into the hall and closed the curtain between them. "I'm not leaving until I find out about Gage."

Yanking off the silly excuse for a hospital gown, she reached for her clothes. Her jeans were passable, but there was no way she was putting on her blood-soaked shirt or jacket.

She stuck her hand between the curtain openings. "Give me your shirt."

"What?"

"Mine's trashed and I'm not modeling the latest push-up bra from Victoria's Secret for the ER. Hand it over. Now."

Seconds later, soft fabric landed in her hand. It was a gray-and-black flannel shirt.

"Thanks."

She tugged it on and buttoned it but didn't bother tucking it in. A scrunchie from her purse held her hair off her face. Grabbing her boots, she opened the curtain again.

"I wasn't suggesting you leave the hospital." Justin held up both hands as if to appease her. "There's a group of people in the waiting room."

"For Gage?"

He nodded. "And for you."

She paused to pull on her boots and blink away the

sudden rush of hot tears. Justin steadied her as she straightened and then surprised her by pulling her into his arms.

"I'm so sorry." He wrapped her in a strong embrace, his shaky words whispered into her hair. "I had no idea what Billy Joe was doing. Please believe me."

Racy leaned into him for a long moment, then stepped back to look at her brother. A rush of sibling love she hadn't felt since she was a little girl filled her. "I believe you."

"Billy Joe is back in custody. Gage wounded him in the leg, but he's going to survive. He'll probably be transferred to the state facility once he's stabilized."

Justin released her, but she kept one arm around his waist as they walked to the waiting room. She didn't want to think about her oldest brother right now. Gage was the only person on her mind. "Is Gage's family here?"

Justin slowed. "Ah, I think the youngest ones are out there. They came in with Leeann, but I didn't see Gina or her mother."

"You didn't see her at the bar? Doesn't she usually work on Tuesdays?"

He shrugged. "I don't know."

"Justin, what aren't you telling me—" Racy stopped as they stepped into the crowded waiting room.

Jackie, one of her assistant managers, sat on a nearby bench with three other waitresses and Ric Murphy, her bouncer. Max headed toward her after giving a steaming cup of coffee to Willie Perkins, one of Maggie's cowboys and Racy's favorite customer.

"What—what are you doing here?" Racy said, flabbergasted.

He stepped forward and enveloped her in his arms. "I had to see for myself you were okay. Damn, you had me worried."

Racy closed her eyes and allowed the strength of his hug to seep into her. "Max! You're supposed to be in Florida."

"I'm supposed to be where I'm needed. I flew home early this morning. I'm needed here. We're all here…for you."

Racy took a deep breath. To know her friends had dropped everything to be here overwhelmed her.

Leeann joined them, stepping away from a circle of people that included a couple of Destiny's deputies. "I was at the end of my shift when the sheriff's call came in. When the on-scene personnel reported his…injuries, I tried to find his mom, but only the twins were home. They said Sandy is in Cheyenne shopping with Gina. We reached them. They're on their way."

Racy spotted Gage's siblings sitting on a nearby couch. The sight of Giselle's red-rimmed eyes and Garrett's clenched fists tore at her heart. She walked over and embraced them.

"Can you tell us anything, Ms. Dillon?" Garrett asked.

Racy wasn't about to share the details of what had happened in the cabin. She glanced at her watch, shocked to see almost three hours had passed since she'd gotten Billy Joe's phone call. "Have the doctors told you anything?"

Giselle shook her head. "We've been here almost an hour and all they've said is they're working to stabilize him."

A doctor in green surgical garb walked into the room.

Racy turned to him, knowing instinctively he was there to see them. "How's Gage?"

The doctor took a moment to look at everyone. "Sheriff Steele is alive, but it doesn't look good."

Her heart stopped beating. She was still conscious, still breathing, but the part of her that belonged to Gage was silently screaming.

"Is there a next of kin here?" the doctor said. "A bullet is lodged near his heart. He's losing blood and we need to get in there and try to stop it. A signed consent form from a family member is needed."

"I'm his brother." Garrett rose. "I'll sign it."

"I need consent from a legal adult. How old are—"

"My mom's still an hour away," he protested. "I'll be eighteen in three months!"

Racy laid a hand on his arm and gave the boy a gentle squeeze, then stepped forward. "I'll sign it. I'm Gage's wife."

Stunned silence filled the room.

"I didn't realize the sheriff was married," the surgeon replied.

Racy felt the weight of everyone's gaze on her as she reached into her purse, but she didn't care. Gage was all that mattered. She rummaged inside, finally pulling out the folded piece of paper. "Here's a copy of our marriage license."

The doctor looked at the paper, then handed Racy a clipboard. "If you'll just sign at the bottom, Mrs. Steele."

A collective gasp and murmurs filled her ears as she penned her name.

"We'll keep you updated as much as we can," the doctor said. "I'm not sure how long the surgery is going to take."

Racy nodded. "Thank you. We'll be here."

The surgeon turned and hurried down the hallway.

She swallowed the lump in her throat, and turned around. Unspoken questions filled the air with a heavy cloud of curiosity. She had to tell them, but first things first.

She went to Garrett and Giselle, humbled when Giselle gripped her hand in a tight squeeze. Racy said, "Your brother and I were married last summer in Vegas."

"Wow."

Racy smiled at Garrett. "Yeah, wow."

"But you didn't tell anyone?" Giselle asked.

"It's a long story."

Racy's gaze connected with Leeann's, whose stunned expression shifted into a compassionate smile. She crouched and took Racy's other hand. "Well, I guess

Maggie was right about you two. She'll be glad to hear your big news."

Racy tried to smile, but she couldn't.

"He's a strong man, Racy." There was certainty in Leeann's voice. "He'll pull through."

The tears she couldn't hold back any longer flooded down her cheeks. "He has to, he just has to."

Chapter Fifteen

It took more strength than he thought he possessed, but Gage finally managed to open his eyes. His throat burned like it was on fire and everything was bright, but hazy. He blinked a few times then realized he was in a hospital.

It all came rushing back.

The hunting cabin. Racy. Billy Joe with a pistol. The sound of gunfire—

Terror and dread filled his chest, cutting off his breath. He struggled to move, to sit up.

"Gage! You're awake. Oh, sweetie, calm down." His mother's soft voice and cool touch invaded his panic.

"Ra—cy…"

"She's fine."

Pain ricocheted in his chest as he turned his head. Eyes squinting, he searched for her familiar red curls and beautiful face. "Where…where is—"

"Considering it's almost five in the morning, she's most

likely asleep in the waiting room. I promise you, she's fine." She squeezed his hand. "We've been taking turns. The hospital only allows two of us in here at a time. Gina just left to get some more coffee."

He looked back at his mother and saw tears in her eyes.

"You gave us quite a scare, young man. It's been the four longest days of my life. You've been breathing on your own for two days now, but waiting for you to wake up after the surgery…" She let her words fade as she brushed at her eyes. "Let me get the nurse. They need to know you're—"

"Wait," he tried to process his mother's words, but it was all a blur. He forced a swallow. "Surgery?"

"Let's wait until the doctor has checked—"

"Mom, please." He forced the words. "I remember…Racy and the cabin…Billy Joe…Jack…firing my weapon…"

"Billy Joe has been taken into custody. He was injured, but survived. Racy and her pup are just fine. Thanks to you."

Relief filled him at her words. He'd never forget the sight of Racy kneeling before her brother, the gun in his shaky grip aimed right at her. Then Billy Joe had raised his arms and Gage had called out, which must have sent Jack into attack mode. Gage had fired, aiming only to wound, not kill. The memory of the blinding pain in his chest caused him to tighten his grip on his mother's hand. "How bad?"

"It was very scary in the beginning. You'd lost a lot of blood and they needed to operate right away. Gina and I weren't—well, thank goodness Racy was here and able to…"

"To what?"

"She signed the consent form." His mother's familiar smile returned, as sweet and serene as he remembered. "As your wife?"

Shocked, he couldn't utter a sound. His heart pounded in his chest, but this time there was no pain, just hope.

It wasn't too late.

"It's true, isn't it?" his mom asked. "She told us you two were married in Las Vegas?"

He nodded. Despite his signature on those damn papers, they were still married. But he had no idea what that meant to Racy, the woman he loved more than life itself.

"Gage, we need to let someone know you're awake. And I want to call the kids and let Racy—"

"Mom…need you to do…something for me."

"Now?"

"Please…at my house." He was determined to do this right this time. "In my top dresser drawer…"

He looked like he was still unconscious.

Even though his mother had insisted Gage had awakened for a few minutes before dawn, he hadn't moved an inch since she'd sat down next to him. His chest rose and fell in an easy rhythm despite the wound that had taken almost eighteen hours to fix.

The longest night of her life.

Racy blinked back tears, amazed that she had any more left.

She'd told an abbreviated story of what had happened in Vegas to everyone, including Gage's family, stressing she and Gage had agreed it had been a mistake and they were taking steps to fix it. Thankfully, Sandy Steele had kept her kids from asking too many questions, and Leeann had provided only quiet support after her assurance had caused Racy to break down and cry.

She'd tried to be strong during the long hours of the operation. It wasn't until the surgeon had assured them Gage would recover that she'd agreed to leave long enough to shower and change. And release a torrent of emotions beneath the hot, stinging spray, finally succumbing to the horror and anguish of all that had happened.

Over the last few days, Billy Joe had been moved to the state hospital in Evanston, and Max had told her to take off as much time as she needed from work. He then surprised her by saying the bank had contacted him, and if she was still interested in owning The Blue Creek, they'd work something out. It wasn't even something she could think about right now, but she was grateful for his offer.

And she'd come to the hospital, staying for hours, waiting for Gage to wake up. She'd lit a candle in the tiny chapel when they were told he was breathing on his own. And now…

Now he was going to be fine.

"You have no idea…" She paused when her tears caused her voice to crack. Thankful for this time alone with him, she knew she had to get through this, so she swallowed and tried again. "I am so sorry, Gage. I never wanted you to be hurt. Please, believe me. I love you…with all my heart."

She pulled the wrinkled paperwork and a pen from her purse. "I know I told myself I'd never say that aloud, but just this once, I wanted to say it…to you…even if you can't hear me. I know I'm not the right woman for you, for so many reasons, and you know that, too, but I'll never forget…"

Using the edge of his hospital bed, she unfolded the paperwork and flipped to the last page. The pen shook and she tightened her grip.

"Not…so…fast."

Racy gasped and looked up. "Gage!"

His blue eyes, shining brightly, looked at her as a small grin creased his lips. His fingers reached out and pulled the papers from her grasp. Shocked, she let them go and watched as he slowly brought up his other hand and ripped the document right down the middle.

"What—what are you doing?"

"You're not," he rasped, pausing to draw in a thin breath, "getting rid of me…that easily."

Her heart, lodged firmly in her throat, made it impossible to speak. Not that she had any idea how to respond. He dropped the torn papers to the floor, and reached out again to grasp her hand. His touch, strong as he curled her fingers in his, broke through her daze.

"Don't do this," she whispered. "We agreed—"

He shook his head and tightened his grip.

"Gage, I'm not what you need. I'm the poster child of bad choices and wrong decisions. I'm headstrong and hot tempered. I act without thinking about the consequences. I get more things wrong than right and I'm—"

"My wife."

The tears spilled from her eyes at his words. The certainty and confidence in his voice broke through her thin resolve. She desperately wanted to believe him. It was all she'd thought about since that moment in the cabin when she'd thought she'd lost him. She wanted to be his wife.

His free hand worked beneath the blankets. Then he pulled out a small black velvet box. He thumbed it open. Her heart jumped when she saw the rings they'd exchanged in Vegas.

He pulled out the smaller of the two, leaving the other in the box resting on his stomach. She allowed him to lift her hand, powerless to stop him as he slid the gold-and-diamond band onto the third finger of her left hand.

"You proposed to me...and I said yes because I've always known I wanted you in my life." His voice grew stronger. "Now I'm asking you to honor those vows and be willing to repeat them before our families and friends. I want you in my house, I want us to make it a home." He held out the velvet box. "I'm asking you to believe in me, in us. I love you, Racy Steele, and I want to be your husband."

Racy brushed away her tears. Could it really be that easy? Could she have what she'd always wanted by simply taking it? By believing in the power of the love she had for this man?

Yes, she could.

She removed the simple gold band and placed it on his finger. "I love you, too, and I want to be your wife. Forever."

He pulled in a deep breath and released it, closing his eyes. A single tear escaped from the corner. "Kiss me, please."

Her mouth trembled as she covered his lips with hers, pouring all her love into a gentle, chaste kiss.

He opened his eyes again, his thumb caressing her wedding band. "You need an engagement ring."

Racy straightened, pulling one hand free to touch his cheek. "I've got you. I don't need anything else."

Gage smiled. "I want you to have one. How about we have one specially made in Paris? I hear it's a great place for a honeymoon."

Happiness filled her soul. She returned his smile. "I think you better concentrate on recovering first."

"I'm taking you to Paris. In the spring. That's a promise."

And Racy knew it was a promise he would keep.

* * * * *

Cherish

BEAUTY AND THE BROODING BOSS *by Barbara Wallace*

Working for author Alex sounds like Kelsey's dream job until she meets her new, rude, unwelcoming boss. Yet beneath his gruff façade could Alex be her Prince Charming?

FRIENDS TO FOREVER *by Nikki Logan*

Marc and Beth were best friends—until a heated kiss exposed secrets and ruined everything. Ten years later, are they ready to forgive the sins of the past?

CROWN PRINCE, PREGNANT BRIDE! *by Raye Morgan*

Monte believed love had no place in his world, until courageous Pellea made him reconsider. Although she's promised to another, he's now determined to fight for her.

VALENTINE BRIDE *by Christine Rimmer*

Reserved Irina was the perfect housekeeper for playboy Caleb. Then she found out she was being deported. So Caleb came up with the ideal solution: marry him!

THE NANNY AND THE CEO *by Rebecca Winters*

CEO Nick can handle billion-dollar business deals with his eyes closed —but a baby? Driven Reese is the perfect nanny, yet could she be something more?

Cherish

**On sale from 4th February 2011
Don't miss out!**

Available at WHSmith, Tesco, ASDA, Eason
and all good bookshops

www.millsandboon.co.uk

THE FAMILY THEY CHOSE
by Nancy Robards Thompson

Struggling to have a baby is shaking Olivia's marriage to the core.
Despite the heartache, Jamison's intent on bringing back his wife's
happiness—one kiss at a time.

PRIVATE PARTNERS
by Gina Wilkins

No one knew about the secret wedding vows Anne had exchanged with
Liam. But now her irresistible husband is back and ready to claim her all
over again.

A COLD CREEK SECRET
by RaeAnne Thayne

Brant is hoping to put the past behind him and find some measure of
solitude and peace at his ranch—but those hopes are dashed when
spoiled heiress Mimi arrives!

RIVA™

Walk on the Wild Side
by Natalie Anderson
Jack Greene has Kelsi throwing caution to the wind—it's hard to stay grounded with a man who turns your world upside down! Until they crash with a bump—of the baby kind...

Do Not Disturb
by Anna Cleary
A preacher's daughter, Miranda was led deliciously astray by wild Joe... Now the tables have turned—he's her CEO! But Joe's polished exterior doesn't disguise his devilish side...

Three Weddings and a Baby
by Fiona Harper
Jennie's groom vanished on their wedding night. When he returns, he has his *toddler* in tow! Jennie can't resist Alex's appeal and, for a successful businesswoman, one kid should be easy...right?

The Last Summer of Being Single
by Nina Harrington
Sebastien Castellano, prodigal city playboy, has mysteriously returned home to his sleepy French village. Now he's reminding single mum Ella how much fun the *single* part can be!

On sale from 4th February 2011
Don't miss out!

Available at WHSmith, Tesco, ASDA, Eason and all good bookshops

www.millsandboon.co.uk

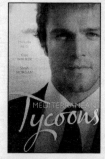

2 FREE BOOKS
AND A SURPRISE GIFT

We would like to take this opportunity to thank you for reading this Mills & Boon® book by offering you the chance to take TWO more specially selected books from the Cherish™ series absolutely FREE! We're also making this offer to introduce you to the benefits of the Mills & Boon® Book Club™—

- **FREE home delivery**
- **FREE gifts and competitions**
- **FREE monthly Newsletter**
- **Exclusive Mills & Boon Book Club offers**
- **Books available before they're in the shops**

Accepting these FREE books and gift places you under no obligation to buy, you may cancel at any time, even after receiving your free books. Simply complete your details below and return the entire page to the address below. You don't even need a stamp!

YES Please send me 2 free Cherish books and a surprise gift. I understand that unless you hear from me, I will receive 5 superb new stories every month, including two 2-in-1 books priced at £5.30 each, and a single book priced at £3.30, postage and packing free. I am under no obligation to purchase any books and may cancel my subscription at any time. The free books and gift will be mine to keep in any case.

Ms/Mrs/Miss/Mr _____ Initials _____

Surname _____

Address _____

_____

_____ Postcode _____

E-mail _____

Send this whole page to: Mills & Boon Book Club, Free Book Offer, FREEPOST NAT 10298, Richmond, TW9 1BR